C.W. POST CENTER - L.I.U.
INSTRUCTIONAL MATERIALS CENTER

The Hammerhead Light

The Hammerhead Light

by Colin Thiele

Harper & Row, Publishers

New York, Hagerstown, San Francisco, London

FIRST AMERICAN EDITION

Library of Congress Cataloging in Publication Data
Thiele, Colin.
  The Hammerhead Light.

  SUMMARY: A lighthouse, a whimbrel, and an old man
help a young girl accept the meaning of change.
  [1. Sea stories. 2. Australia—Fiction.
3. Lighthouses—Fiction] I. Title.
PZ7.T354Ham3   [Fic]   76-24311
ISBN 0-06-026116-1
ISBN 0-06-026117-X lib. bdg.

To the great lighthouses and their keepers

The Hammerhead Light

One

About a hundred people lived in the little town of Snapper Bay in southern Australia. Some of them were young, and some were old, and some were in-between.

Axel Jorgensen was seventy-two, with a mop of white hair and a cotton-wool beard, and legs that bowed outward like bananas. He looked something like Father Christmas.

Tessa Noble was twelve, with a mop of brown hair and tapioca-freckled cheeks, and legs that bowed inward at the knees like bent sticks. She lived in a white house in the main street of Snapper Bay. There was only one street in the whole town, so it had to be the main one anyway. She lived with her father and mother and her grown-up brother, Jody, and Jody's wife, Bridget.

Axel Jorgensen lived by himself in a wooden hut far around the curve of the bay, away from the town. It was the place where the sandy beach ended and the first rocks reared up near the start of the Hammerhead Handle. He was a fisherman and a forager, a boatman and a beachcomber, a talker and a teacher. He taught Tessa many things. When they walked along the coast together he taught her about seashells and albatrosses, and when they walked inland by the lakes and marshes he taught her about summer sedges, snails, and spoonbills in the wildlife sanctuary. She thought he was one of the Wise Men of the World.

She had called him Uncle Axel for as long as she could remember, even though they were not related. He often came to have a meal in Tessa's house, and Tessa's father went fishing with him whenever he could. She spent as much time pottering about near his shack as she did in her own little street in Snapper Bay.

The shack was filled with things that Tessa's mother called junk. There were oars and rusty oarlocks, bits of rope, rudder pins and grappling hooks, boxes, chains, and old craypots that seemed ancient enough to have come out of Noah's Ark. For Axel had been a sailor as well as a beachcomber, a lighthouse keeper as well as a fisherman. He had known Tessa since the day she was born.

Axel loved all living things—even Rump, the young wombat, who caused him a lot of trouble. Rump had been run over by a car near the Murray River, and the driver had picked him up and left him with Axel, just like a patient in a hospital. When Rump had recovered he had stayed on, burrowing in the bank behind the hut or wandering down to the town to thin out someone's vegetable garden.

"It's that potbellied wombat again," people used to

2

say when they found out. "Take him back to Axel."

And so Rump would soon be back digging in his bank again or snuffling in a corner of the hut or scrabbling under the floor. Once Axel had disappeared completely into a new wombat hole while he had been stirring the porridge at the stove. But he was never angry with Rump. He wouldn't even call him a pet. He was a mate, he said, a friend and a companion.

One morning when Tessa walked around the long curve of the beach to Axel's hut she found him busy and excited. He was working at the vise on his bench near the door of his shack.

"What are you doing?" she asked. "What's up?"

"You'll never guess, Tessa girl," he said. She knew that something had happened, because he never called her Tessa girl unless he was excited.

"What is it, then?"

"Look inside." He nodded his head at the shack. "But move slowly."

She was suspicious and walked very carefully. "Is it a snake?"

"Not a snake. Come and see."

At first she couldn't see anything at all in the shadow. She opened her eyes wide and then puckered them quickly to get a clearer view.

"I can't see a thing."

"Not very smart, are you?" He chuckled. "Wouldn't take you out to see things in the marshes."

"Is it a . . . Oh!" Suddenly she saw it. There was a little silence while she took a breath and looked at it. Axel went on working busily at the vise on his bench.

3

It was a bird with a long curved beak, lying on its side in a large wire cage, panting. It was streaked brown and buff over the wings and body, but its breast was white and its crown had long white stripes above the eyes. It was beautiful—lovely mottled feathers and bright frightened eyes, and a long slender downward-curving bill.

"What is it?" Tessa asked at last.

Axel straightened up and stopped his filing at the vise. "A whimbrel," he said.

"A whimbrel." Tessa tasted the name on her tongue. "I like that. It's a name with meanings in the sounds."

"Yes," Axel answered. "Speed and distance, and lonely faraway cries in the night."

Tessa paused and looked at it again. "Is it hurt?"

"Yes."

She sensed something in his voice. "Is it very bad?"

"Pretty bad."

"Wings?" she asked.

Axel took the thing he was making out of the vise, examined it, put it back, and turned toward her.

"He's lost a foot, Tessa. He can't stand up properly."

She was horrified. "A foot? How on earth could he have lost a foot?"

"Who knows?"

"A fish? Do you think maybe a barracuda bit it off?"

Axel shook his head. "It would have happened on the land—or in the air. He likes the inlets and the mud flats."

"A sharp piece of iron, then? Or a piece of wire—a power line he didn't see when he was flying fast?"

4

Axel's big mop of white hair trembled as he shook his head again. "No. A bullet, more likely."

Tessa was appalled. "Not a bullet!" she said quickly. "Nobody would shoot at a whimbrel!"

"No?" Axel rubbed angrily with a file. "Have you seen the way Tiny Herbert or Joe Zucci handle a rifle around here? Like maniacs!"

"But not at a whimbrel. Surely they wouldn't shoot at a whimbrel."

"They'd shoot at anything. At a stilt or a curlew or an ibis or a pelican, at a spoonbill or a snipe or a swallow or a swan, at a post or a tin or a light bulb or a tank. They ought to be locked up."

"That's awful." She was silent for a while. "What's going to happen to him?"

Old Axel looked up sharply. "What do you think? He can't live as he is, can he? He has to fly all the way to Siberia or Canada in a few weeks' time."

"But that's on the other side of the world!"

"Yes. Big enough trip to tackle with two legs."

She sat on an old box near the door and glanced back and forth from Axel to the whimbrel. "Can he land on one foot, and take off again?"

"Most birds can stand on one foot—if it's not too windy. But his other foot is hurt too—the claw."

"Can't he stand at all, then?"

"He can tumble about and hop and flap and flop. But how could he live like that? How could he get enough food? It would be better to put him away than to let him starve to death."

Her eyes opened wide. "Put him away?"

"Yes. Kill him kindly."

"No," she said quickly. "Oh no, you wouldn't do that." She paused for a second and looked at the old man shrewdly. "You couldn't do that, could you?"

He seemed to be so busy at his vise that at first she thought he hadn't heard her. But after a while he went on without looking up. "Sometimes things have to be done even when you don't want to do them. Even when it's very hard."

"I know you wouldn't do it," she said confidently, "even if you could." She stood up and went over to him. "What are you making?"

He unfastened something very small from the vise and held it up. It was a foot. A tiny wooden foot—for a whimbrel.

Two

Tessa held the whimbrel while Axel tried to fit the artificial foot. It was not an easy thing to do, even though the little piece of wood was carefully made, with three carved toes, and a hollow stem to fit over the stump of the leg.

Fortunately the whimbrel didn't struggle. Axel showed Tessa how to hold it firmly and gently with the wings wrapped against its body. Although it was frightened it seemed to know that they were trying to help. Its dark eyes blinked and flashed, and when its head moved jerkily its long bill darted about like a probe. Tessa was spellbound.

"It must be four inches long," she said.

Axel didn't even look up. "Four!" he said. "More like sixteen; nice streamlined bird, the whimbrel."

"Not the bird. The bill."

"What about the bill?"

"It must be four inches long."

"The bill is, yes. Not the bird."

"No, the bill, the bill."

"Well, why didn't you say so in the first place?"

Tessa snorted. "Really, Uncle Axel!" She was about to say much more, but decided to hold her peace. She looked down at the whimbrel again, at the great curving beak, as black as ebony, at the white breast, the mottled back, and the light stripe running above the eyebrows and over the curve of his head.

"Oh, you're a beautiful fellow," she said. But the bird suddenly struggled and she had to tighten her grip.

"Hold still, Willie," said old Axel gently. "We've nearly finished."

"Is that his name—Willie?"

"Suits him, I reckon. Will-he walk? Or won't he?"

"*Will-he* walk! That's a dreadful joke, Uncle Axel."

"Well, we'll soon know."

"Finished?"

"Finished."

Axel put his pliers and other tools aside and straightened up. "Put him down in his pen."

The whimbrel fluttered for a minute, but he settled down quickly and began to pace up and down in the cage. At first he lifted his leg with a high awkward step like a man learning to walk on skis, but before long he grew used to it and stomped about happily. Tessa had her nose pressed against the wire. "It works, Uncle Axel," she said excitedly. "It actually works."

"Of course it works," he answered haughtily.

"D'you think he'll be able to fly now, and land without somersaulting?"

"Give him a day or two to get used to it," Axel said. "It's not every day that a bird has to learn to fly with a wooden leg."

It was wise to wait. Two days later the wooden leg was useless. After Willie had walked in his tray of water a few times the light wood grew soggy and began to break up.

"Fat lot of use that was, Willie," said Axel. "Wouldn't have lasted you to Mount Gambier, let alone to the other side of the world. We'll have to do better than that."

So he worked at his bench for another whole day and made a metal foot—of aluminum. It was beautifully shaped, but it was too hard to fit to Willie's leg.

"Won't work," Axel admitted at last. "Might hurt him; probably do more harm than good."

Tessa was downhearted. "Whatever are we going to do, then? He looks so helpless when you take his foot away from him."

"We'll win yet. I've still got bags of ideas."

This time he made a plastic foot, cutting the shape carefully to match the real one, and melting out a hollow stem with a red-hot skewer. It fitted beautifully. But Axel was still not satisfied. He experimented for another two days, making more and more little feet and varying the length and diameter of the hollow stem until he had one that was perfect. It fitted snugly over the whole of the stump of Willie's leg and extended a half inch or so beyond it so that the two legs—the real one and the artificial one—were of exactly the same length. Then Axel fastened a tiny clamp around the stump to be doubly sure.

9

"Now, Willie," he said, "you ought to be able to dance to music."

Willie walked as if he was marching in a brass band. He looked so pleased that Tessa thought his big bill would break out into a long downward-curving smile.

"He's all right this time," she said. "Now he really can look after himself."

Axel kept him for another week, checking the foot carefully every day. By now Willie was quite tame, standing quietly when they came near him and even eating out of their hands. Tessa could see that Axel was becoming so fond of him that soon he wouldn't be able to part with him.

"Are you going to keep Willie?" she asked slyly one day. "Or are you going to set him free?"

Axel looked at her quizzically.

Tessa was very uncomfortable. She knew she had been rude and she was certain that he knew it too.

"Come on then," he said suddenly, lifting Willie out of his cage. "It's time you tested your new foot out in the wide world."

They carried the whimbrel inland over the dunes behind the shack until they came to the open flats beyond Snapper Bay. Then they stopped and both of them looked at Willie for the last time. His dark eyes were flashing and blinking. Tessa felt very sad, as if she was about to say farewell to a special friend forever.

"Good-bye, Willie," she whispered. "Look after yourself."

"Off you go," said Axel. "You'll be all right now."

He put Willie down on the firm clay near the edge of

the mud flats. Willie stood for a second or two as if he was amazed at the sight of everything around him. Then he ran forward for a few steps and rose easily into the air. They both stood watching, holding their hands up to shade their eyes.

"Just look at him fly," Tessa said, "so fast and free."

"Beautiful," said Axel, watching intently. "Beautiful fellow."

They both remained with their hands to their eyes until the whimbrel curved downward at last toward the skyline by the marshes and they lost sight of him. Though the world was full of birds it was suddenly empty.

"Back home, Tessa," said Axel gently. He saw her eyes misting over and her lip trembling. "No need to be sad for Willie," he said quietly. "He's happy back with the other whimbrels—with all his friends. It wouldn't be right to keep him in a cage, especially when they all fly to the other side of the world. Think how lonely he would be then. You wouldn't like that."

She shook her head. "No, I wouldn't like that."

"And think what a hero he'll be. He'll be able to talk about his wooden leg for the rest of his life."

"His plastic leg."

"Just like old Mrs. Elliot with her operation."

Tessa smiled. "He will be sort of special, won't he?"

"Super special," said Axel. "There won't be another whimbrel like him in the whole world."

Three

Tessa was sad. She was thinking about Willie Whimbrel, about a frail bird facing a fearful journey across the world—perhaps getting weaker and weaker, perhaps being left behind by the rest of his companions to die in a strange place.

But it went deeper than that. She was sad for all things that were hurt or handicapped, sad for parting, sad for loneliness, sad for the loss of friends. Sad for herself.

She was mooching along the shore far to the west of Snapper Bay. It was something she often did when she felt sad and wanted to be alone. She would get up early in the morning and walk and walk. She never really knew how far she went—six miles, eight, ten. But it didn't matter. Time and distance were not important.

She loved the sound of the sea on the shells and gritty beaches, like seething soda water in a glass. She liked the wind on her cheeks, the sand and pebbles underfoot, the cry of the seabirds, and the colors of the sunrise in the sky. She liked the feeling of space and solitude and pure endless air; she felt as if she could dip her body in it and cool her heart until the ache dwindled and died away.

She was on her way back, heading steadily along the coast toward the cliffs of Hammerhead Point. The shore was so rugged now that she had to leave the waterline and pick her way upward among the rocks and ledges to the flat tableland above. It was hard work for a while and she was panting steadily by the time she reached the top. She wondered whether it was past breakfast time, and whether her mother would be calling loudly and angrily at the back door.

She had taken only a few steps along the upper track when she stopped and peered ahead. Something was going on at the Hammerhead Light. A snub-nosed Land Rover was standing at the edge of the cliffs and two men were walking down the Handle toward the lighthouse tower. When they reached it they took out a reel of measuring tape and started walking about, taking measurements and calculating heights and distances.

Tessa ran forward quickly and silently. As she reached the Land Rover she could see a crest painted on the cabin door, and the words MARINE AND HARBORS painted in an arc above it. Immediately she was suspicious, but because there was no hope of crossing the Handle without being seen she put on a bold front and walked openly toward the men.

"Hullo," she said as she came up.

The two men paused, eyeing her.

"Good day," they both said. They looked very much alike, except that one of them was wearing a beret and the other one a felt hat. There was a brief silence.

"Out walking the dog?" Beret asked.

"Haven't got a dog."

"Taking a constitutional then?"

Tessa wrinkled her nose, nonplussed. "Taking a what?"

"A walk—to keep fit."

"Oh, in a way I guess."

She looked at them sharply—at the tape measure, at the notebook and pencil which Felt Hat was holding in his hands.

"What are you doing?"

"Taking some measurements."

"What for?"

"To make some calculations."

She didn't like them. She felt uneasy, as if they were playing cat and mouse with her.

"Why do you keep on messing about with the tower?" she blurted out suddenly and angrily. "Why can't you leave it alone?"

Beret looked at her calmly. "Because it's not safe to be left alone anymore. One day the peninsula will crash headlong into the sea—head, neck, tower, and all. The Hammerhead Light should be demolished before it becomes a menace to everyone. It's dangerous."

"You're always saying that. You said that the last time you were here."

"It's true—more true this time than last time."

"Why is it?"

14

"The tower's listing and cracking."

"What do you mean, listing?"

Felt Hat took his pencil and drew a quick sketch on a blank page of his book. "It's tilting," he said, pointing to the sketch. "Like that. It's canting off the vertical. Leaning toward the sea."

Beret took the tape measure and a pencil, and began to make black marks on the tower near the level of his shoulder.

"We'll need to knock out fifteen or twenty feet of stone on this side," he said to Felt Hat. "But all the charges will have to fire together if the whole thing's going to settle down neatly."

"If they don't," answered Felt Hat, "it'll be like granny's false teeth when she dropped them on the concrete."

Tessa's eyes opened wide with disbelief.

"You're going to blow up the tower!" she exclaimed. She was so aghast that she didn't know whether they replied or not. "You are, aren't you?"

They watched her, startled by the expression on her face, the accusing tone in her voice.

"Well," said Beret a little sheepishly.

"Not now," answered Felt Hat. "We're only making a report."

Tessa couldn't talk to them any longer. She backed away, as she would have backed away from something dangerous. The men from Adelaide had never understood what the lighthouse meant to the town. Old Axel Jorgensen said that this was because they used their heads and not their hearts, and because they lived

15

jammed up together in a big heap in Adelaide, like a clump of chicken lice. They had never seen the Hammerhead Light in the twilight with the full moon balanced on top of it like a monstrous golden orange; they had never seen the tower at midnight, as black as coal against the scudding clouds and the gloom; they had never seen it gleaming brightly in the summer sunrise. They had never lived in Snapper Bay. Tessa turned and raced along the Handle toward Axel's hut. She sped down the steep path toward the hollow above the beach where the hut nestled.

"Uncle Axel! Uncle Axel!" she yelled when she was still fifty yards away. "Come quickly!"

She rocketed up to the door and burst into the dim kitchen. "Uncle Axel!" But there was nobody in the hut. She ran outside again, glancing desperately to left and right. "Uncle Axel!" Silence everywhere. He must have gone into Snapper Bay to get a few things from the shop.

So she set out around the long curve of the beach—over a mile of sand and seaweed—to raise the alarm in the town. Before long her heart was thumping in her ears and she had a strange sweet taste in her mouth, as if her lungs were leaking blood. But she ran on. Her breath came in big gulps—half sob, half gasp—and her legs started to waver. But still she ran on. Her eyes watered, not from the wind alone, but from fear and frustration. And so at last she reached the break at the end of the beach, ran panting past the jetty and the rusting winch on the shore, and lurched up the little street to the white gate in front of her father's house.

16

She fumbled with the latch for a second, then stumbled through the front door.

They were all in the kitchen—her mother and father, her brother, Jody, and his wife, Bridget.

And right at the head of the table, like an old grandfather of the family, sat Uncle Axel with a big cup of tea in his hands.

"Uncle Axel!" Tessa said, panting and wheezing in the doorway. "I've . . . I've been looking for . . . for you all over."

"Easy, Tess," said Jody. "You'll burst your boiler."

Her mother looked afraid. "What's the matter?" she asked quickly. "Has someone been hurt?"

They were all staring at her from the breakfast table.

"The Hammerhead Light," Tessa gasped. "They're going to blow it up."

Her father stood up with a jerk. "The devil they are!" he said.

"Blow it up?" Jody said disbelievingly. "Who are?"

"Two men. In a Land Rover."

"With dynamite?"

"With . . . with lots of charges. On one side."

Her father walked over to her sternly. "Who told you this?"

"The men did. I watched them. They were measuring the tower to get it ready."

Everyone was so busy talking that nobody noticed old Axel, who had slipped out through the back door as quick as a dervish and was heading back to his shack. By the time Tessa and her father and Jody caught up with him he was halfway home.

"Don't rush so much," Jody called. "You'll have a heart attack."

But Axel took no notice. He was mumbling in his beard, muttering all kinds of things about blasted vermin, gangsters, and lice from Adelaide. They knew what he meant.

As soon as Axel reached his shack he rushed inside, seized his shotgun, and then headed out for the Hammerhead. The others followed him.

"Steady now, Axel," Tessa's father said. "Don't lose your head."

"I won't lose mine," Axel answered grimly.

"There could be an accident."

"It won't be an accident. Don't you worry."

"Better give me the gun."

"D'you think I can't shoot straight? I get me a rabbit twice a week."

"These aren't rabbits."

"Darn sure they're not rabbits. They're dingoes, foxes, weasels."

In the end Mr. Noble had to run ahead and block the entrance to the Hammerhead Handle so that nobody could get past. Even then it looked as if old Axel was going to rush at him and force his way through, but he gave up his gun at last, rumbling and thundering like an old volcano. Then they all marched on together toward the villains at the Hammerhead Light.

18

Four

It took a week for the town to recover. The two men went back to Adelaide without blowing up the tower, but everyone in Snapper Bay was suspicious of them.

"They'll come back," said Axel. "They'll come back. You'll see." So the fishermen set up a watch during the night and their wives kept guard during the day. Tessa acted as a messenger.

"If they come back," said fat Mrs. Snelling, "we'll give them ants in their pants."

The other women laughed and nodded.

"Buckshot in their britches."

"We'll lie down in front of their wheels."

"Let down their tires."

"Stuff rags up their exhaust pipe."

"Chew their ears off."

In Adelaide the two men reported back to their headquarters. "The mood of the town is ugly," they said. "If we're going to blow up the tower, we'll need police to protect us."

"It's just a storm in a teacup," said the director. "It'll soon pass over when the hotheads all cool down."

There were some people in the town who agreed that it was a lot of fuss about nothing. Tessa's mother was one of them.

"Why bother about a worm-eaten old lighthouse?" she asked. "It's on its last legs anyway."

"Because it's ours," said Tessa. "Because it belongs to Snapper Bay."

"Because it's history," said Jody. "Because it goes back to the early days."

"Because it's beautiful," said Bridget.

"And useful," said Mr. Noble. "It has saved hundreds of boats from shipwreck and thousands of men from drowning."

"Because it stands for something," said old Axel loudly. "It's a sign. It stands for help and strength and watchfulness. No matter what winds come up from the south, or what rains come thundering down from heaven, when the clouds clear and the spume spins away there it is again. Night or day, darkness or light, the tower stands there like a sentinel—something to lift up our eyes to, something to make us feel safe and strong."

"That's it exactly," said Tessa, clapping and cheering.

"Codswallop!" said Tessa's mother. "A lot of sentimental claptrap."

. She was thin-faced and clear-eyed, with faint marks on her skin like traces of old freckles. People said she was a strong-willed woman who liked to call a spade a spade. Sometimes when Uncle Axel was angry with Tessa he told her that she was as headstrong and as

20

stubborn as her mother, and then Tessa didn't know whether he was giving out praise or insults. The other women in the town always said that Tessa looked exactly like her mother; even her father joked about it and said she was a chip off mum's block. Tessa couldn't understand it. She didn't think she was anything like her mother, who was old-faced and sharp-tongued and grown-up. And their feelings about things were quite different.

"The lighthouse is a rickety lump of limestone," her mother was saying. "It's nothing more than that."

"It's a historic landmark," Jody answered.

"It has saved thousands of lives," Mr. Noble repeated.

"It's magic in the moonlight," Tessa said.

"And ghostly in the gloom," Bridget added.

"And nobody is going to harm it," Axel said firmly, "even if I have to guard it for twenty years."

Tessa laughed. "You'll be ninety-two by then, Uncle Axel, and your beard will be down to your knees."

"And my blunderbuss will still be as good as new," he answered ominously.

Another week went by and the hubbub over the lighthouse died away.

"We still should have someone on guard," Jody said one morning at breakfast. "Someone to keep watch all day and night."

"We can't keep watch forever," his father said. "There aren't enough people in the town. In any case, I think the trouble is over now. Those fellows in Adelaide all know how we feel."

21

Mr. Noble was kindhearted and easygoing. He liked to give people the benefit of the doubt. But Jody and Tessa were as sharp as their mother.

"I wouldn't trust them," Jody grumbled.

"Neither would I," Tessa agreed. "The one with the beret had a face like a ferret."

And then suddenly the problem was solved. The first of the year's autumn storms came roaring over the coast, making mad-dog noises and rattling the town like a dishful of bones. The chimney of the schoolhouse was blown down and Mr. Perkins, the headmaster, nearly had his toes crushed when a barrowload of bricks came thundering into the fireplace. The verandah of the post office collapsed and three pine trees near the foreshore were tilted over at such an angle that they looked like big guns aimed at the second story of the Grand Hotel. But nobody knew about the most important effect of all until the following day. And the first one to find out was Tessa.

It was nine o'clock on a Saturday morning when she came larruping around the bay to visit Axel in his shack. She ran with her arms held out like wings, swooping and curving and skimming over the heaps of foam that had been flung up on the sand by the storm. She called out to the sea gulls as if she was one of them, and teased the albatrosses. The storm clouds were breaking up and racing away to the east and the sunlight flared and faded and flared again, mottling the beach with patches of sunshine and shadow. The world was crisp and newly washed, and she was part of it—she and the wild creatures and all the people of the little town.

Tessa ran on, fast and free. She was full of energy and life. Sometimes, these days, she felt that it was exciting just to be alive, as if her whole body was stirring, ready to burst out of its skin.

"Hullo, sea gull," she called loudly to a proud fellow who was standing in the shallow ripples with his head pointing into the wind. "Got a clean bib on today?" And then she stopped short in her tracks and stood staring.

She had almost rounded the arc of the bay to the point where the sand hills ended and Axel's shack nestled in the last little nook before the rocks began and the shore reared up into the cliffs of the Hammerhead Handle.

But there was no shack to be seen. No breakfast smoke on the morning air. Not even a chimney. Only a rubbish dump in the hollow, a mess of old roofing iron scattered all over the sand hills, and a jumble of furniture, household junk, and crushed craypots lying under a heap of broken timber.

Tessa ran forward. "Uncle Axel!" she cried. "Oh, no! Uncle Axel!"

She rushed down into the hollow, plunging over the twisted iron and splintered wood, calling and searching. "Uncle Axel! Uncle Axel!" But there was no answer. If the old man was still nearby he was not within earshot. Or perhaps he was lying unconscious under the wreckage of his hut.

Tessa crawled to the middle of the mess, heaving aside broken rafters and hauling at sheets of roofing iron. "Uncle Axel!" she kept calling desperately. "Can you hear me?" But Uncle Axel didn't hear.

At last she stopped her frantic search and sat down

23

exhausted on the end of a broken joist. A sob welled up in her throat. She looked about blankly at the empty sand hills, at the long curve of the bay, at the town beyond it. She would have to raise the alarm—run exhausted up the main street yelling to everyone that the storm had flattened Axel's hut and somehow spirited him away.

"Cooee!"

It was so clear on the breeze that Tessa leaped up, tingling and alert.

"Cooee, Tessa girl!"

It was Uncle Axel's voice, as clear as a bell. And nobody else ever called her Tessa girl.

"Hullo," she yelled. "Uncle Axel! Uncle Axel!"

"Cooee!"

It was above her. It was in the air somewhere, coming down to her like the high piping of a bird. She scanned the sand hills urgently, and then the rocks beyond the hollow.

"Tessa girl!"

At last she saw him—up on the cliffs at the start of the Hammerhead Handle, waving his arms like a windmill, though they seemed no bigger than the hands of a clock. She waved and shouted back, and he beckoned her toward him.

It was some time before she reached him—clambering up the track like a rock wallaby and rushing up to him at last, her forehead wet with perspiration and her chest heaving.

"Uncle Axel! What on earth are you doing up here?"

His white beard streamed in the wind and his eyes

24

twinkled. He looked more like Father Christmas than ever. "Come with me," he said.

She hung back, questioning. "What happened? Did the storm blow down the hut?"

"Roof, walls, and chimney. Clean sweep. Took the lot."

"You could have been killed."

"Need more than a puff of wind to do that, Tessa girl."

"It must have been awful."

"Best bit of luck I ever had."

"Why?"

"I'll show you. Come on."

He led her across the causeway, leaning forward against the wind and holding her hand tightly. The breeze was still biting over the cliffs. It flattened Tessa's blouse against her body and tore at her hair. She turned her face into it just as the sea gulls did, but then it started to stifle her breath and chafe tears from her eyes.

"Here," said Axel at last. "Look!"

They had reached the place where the tower of the great lighthouse rose up in front of them. It seemed the same as ever, except for one thing. The heavy wooden door that had been bolted and locked for so long was standing open. Axel led Tessa inside.

"How did you do it?" she asked, looking around slowly. "When . . . ?"

"This morning," he said, chuckling. "First thing this morning."

"But . . ."

"Had to do something, didn't I? Shack was gone. Nowhere to live. And the wind was mighty cold."

"But how did you do it?"

"Get inside?"

"Yes."

"Didn't break the door down, did I?"

He seemed to be enjoying himself more and more. His cheeks were rosy and his eyes sparkled. "Didn't pick the lock. Didn't write to Adelaide on official paper and say, 'Dear Sir, Please can I live in the lighthouse because my shack's gone with the wind?'" He was laughing out loud now, his shoulders shaking gently with the joy of it all.

"How, then?"

He leaned forward as if about to whisper a secret in her ear. "Just took the old key I had hanging by the fireplace ever since I worked here thirty years ago."

"You had a key all the time?"

He was hugging himself with both arms. "For thirty years. So I just unlocked the door and walked in." And he laughed until little tears sparkled in the creases of his eyes.

Tessa looked around carefully. "It's a lovely place to stay."

The room at the bottom of the tower was a circle eight or nine yards across, with a low ceiling and a potbellied old stove against the wall. In one place a steel ladder ran up through a hatch in the ceiling to a landing above them. It all looked very snug. Already Axel had carried some of his things up from the wrecked shack, and he was plainly planning to bring some more.

26

"The walls are thick," he said. "It's snugger than a hole in your socks."

"Yes," said Tessa, "but what about the men from Adelaide?"

"They're lice," said Axel contemptuously.

"They won't let you stay."

"First they'll have to get me out," he said, grinning wickedly.

She looked about the room again and nodded. "You're right, Uncle Axel. If you shut the door they couldn't get in."

"Not a hope," he said. "I could pour molasses down on their heads from the lookout."

"And you could keep watch—all the time." Tessa began to understand his plan. "Now the people of the town will always have someone on guard up here."

He chuckled and nodded. "Someone to give the alarm."

She looked at him shrewdly. "But how will you let them know?"

"I'll need a messenger," he answered. "Someone with sharp eyes, who can run fast."

"Yes," she said, smiling. "You will."

Five

Axel soon settled in. The next day the big circular room at the bottom of the tower looked like a rummage sale in a whirlwind, but it was a snug, happy place all the same. Tessa wished she could have had a place like it for herself, but there was no hope of that.

Outside on the seaward side of the tower was a small yard surrounded by a white stone wall. Here Axel set up his workbench and his wooden seats and a lot of other odds and ends that were too big or too clumsy to fit inside. Tessa's father helped him carry the heavier pieces across the Handle from the wreck of the shack; they would laugh and joke about it at the start of each trip, but by the time they reached the tower they were wheezing like a couple of old cows with colic. Then they would have to rest while Axel made a cup of tea to get over it.

"You're a hoarder," said Tessa's father when they

had finished the last trip. "You're worse than a bower-bird."

"I never waste things," Axel answered.

"What about pig bristles and hair clippings?"

Axel chuckled. "You should never cut your hair. Makes you weak. Look what happened to Samson."

Tessa and her father laughed too. Then, because it was a fine day with warm sunshine and a calm sea, they all went outside and walked to the end of the Hammerhead.

It was like standing on the edge of the world. The cliffs plunged down at their feet and the far plain of the sea stretched away toward the horizon and bent slowly out of sight around the great curve of the earth. Someone seemed to have smashed a million mirrors and flung the bits onto the water where they shivered with needle-pricks of light that darted straight at Tessa's eyes. The sea was so peaceful that even the Dragon's Mouth—a vicious place with a million teeth that tore at the hull of a boat like a chip mill mauling a log; where the waves boiled yeastily day and night—had exchanged its roar for a sleepy hiss.

A white crayboat was coming down The Narrows, making for Snapper Bay. It swung past Anvil Rock (where the men from Adelaide had placed the smart new automatic beacon that replaced the Hammerhead Light), the skipper standing at the tiller with the faint sea breeze in his hair, and the rest of the crew sitting on the deck in the sunshine. They saw the three figures on the cliffs and waved as the boat passed under the headland.

29

"Fine day all right," said Tessa's father. "Old Buberic isn't even wearing his cap."

Axel nodded. "Most other days he would lose his ears."

They walked on around the edge of the Hammerhead. On the seaward side they suddenly stopped.

"Look at that," Mr. Noble said, pointing at his feet.

A big crack, six or eight inches wide, ran inland from the edge, stretching on and on, gradually growing thinner until it was no more than a line like a strand of hair. But by that time it had almost reached the other side of the Hammerhead.

"Those fellows from Adelaide were right," Tessa's father went on. "The Hammerhead is cracking up. This must have happened in that last big storm."

Axel tossed his head and stroked his beard as he always did when he wanted to show that he didn't care a cent about the argument, or didn't even believe it.

"It's been doing that for a thousand years," he said, "and I reckon it'll still be doing it for a thousand more."

But Mr. Noble was very serious. "Have a look at those sea stacks farther down the coast," he said. "They were just like the Hammerhead once. Now they're islands out in the sea, or big dumps of rock lying smashed up at the bottom of the cliffs."

Axel continued to swish about with his beard, holding it with his right hand and flicking the end impatiently like a horse swatting flies.

"You worry too much, Harry," he said. "Are you sure your house isn't going to fall down tonight? What about

30

the chimney? I didn't like the look of it the last time I saw it."

"Well," said Mr. Noble. "Don't blame me if the tower falls down on top of you."

"It won't do that unless those fellows from Adelaide come crawling around again with their dynamite."

Tessa could see that her father was getting impatient and that Uncle Axel was getting stubborn.

"It's time we went home," she said quickly. "Mum will be wondering where we are."

Her father gave her a speculative look and smiled. "I think you're right, Tessa. We should be going."

So they said good-bye to Axel and left him swishing his beard. Then Tessa put her hand inside her father's where she could feel the big rough grip of his palm, and they walked off together around the coast to Snapper Bay.

Axel had been living in the Hammerhead Lighthouse for a couple of weeks before Tessa discovered something new. It was a gray Saturday morning with a cold wind whistling over the headland. She was sitting in the snug round room, glad to be inside at last after her long walk around the beach.

"Uncle Axel," she said, looking about quickly, "you haven't got a bed. Where on earth do you sleep?"

He chuckled. "Don't need a bed. Sleep standing up."

She scoffed. "Come on, Uncle Axel. Where is it?"

He beckoned her and they walked over to the iron ladder that led up through the trapdoor in the ceiling.

"Come with me," he said secretively, "and I'll show

you something." They climbed through to the landing and stood together for a minute, looking about. Tessa drew her breath. "Wowee, Uncle Axel! It's better than the last one."

They were standing in another room, smaller than the one below them but even cozier. Axel's bunk, a locker for his clothes, and a small table stood near the wall in one spot, and other things were scattered about the floor —knee boots, a packet of candles, an old telescope, a lantern, some newspapers, and a few books. Three narrow slit windows shielded by thick glass looked out over the headland. But the most striking thing of all was a narrow spiral staircase that seemed to grow right out of the floor in the middle of the room and go winding up and up so far toward heaven that Tessa grew dizzy just from trying to trace its path. And running down the center of the spiral, like the pendulum of an old grandfather clock, was a steel cable that ended in a clump of heavy weights.

Tessa puckered her eyes and wrinkled her nose as she gazed up and up. "It's so *high*," she said. "From the outside I didn't dream that it was as high as this."

He chuckled knowingly. "You haven't seen anything," he said. "Do you feel sprightly enough to climb a bit?"

"If you do," she answered.

"Better not look down," he said. "Some people get dizzy."

She waited while he climbed the first few steps of the staircase and then followed closely behind him. She marveled at his speed. Here she was, young and bursting with energy, but it was all she could do to keep up with him. And he was nearly seventy-three.

They passed two more landings that led into rooms like the ones below them. They seemed to be store-rooms, still partly filled with odds and ends—cans of kerosene and methyl alcohol, old tools, a box marked MANTLES, packets of various kinds, and even an old oilcan.

"You'd think they would have cleared all this up before they left," said Tessa. "It's just a mess."

"They were told to leave it. A gang was going to be sent from Adelaide."

"To clean up?"

"To strip the light and make a list of everything before they knocked down the tower."

"But they didn't come?"

"No, because the people of Snapper Bay stopped them."

"But they're sure to come back in the end."

"Of course. But now I'm in here like an old weasel in a hole."

He chuckled gleefully and went on climbing. Tessa followed. She was panting hard by now, and little drops of perspiration stood out on her forehead. She wondered how much higher they could possibly climb without suddenly popping out above the clouds, when at last the stairs ended and they were standing in a small dome-shaped room at the very top of the tower. It was dim and gloomy and the room was partly filled with strange machinery. For a moment she was half afraid. This was the place where, for more than a hundred years, the great light had flashed out to warn ships and sailors about the perils of rocks and cliffs.

This was the place where men had toiled and waited and watched to see that the light never went out at night—not once, not even for a minute, in a hundred years. Until now.

"Just a second," said Axel, "while I take down the curtains."

Tessa was more astonished than ever. "Curtains?" she said. "Up here?"

"Not for the reason you think."

"What then?"

"To stop the sunlight getting into the lenses and causing a fire."

She opened her eyes wide. "How could it?"

"You'll see. You've got a lot to learn about lighthouses."

Although it was gray and cloudy outside, the daylight filled the place as soon as the curtains came down, and Tessa could see things plainly. The center of the light was actually a mantle just like the ones on the big pressure lamp her father used when he went fishing on the beach at night. When the burner underneath it was very hot the kerosene that was fed in under pressure turned into vapor and ignited, and then the mantle glowed with a pure white light. But even so Tessa could not imagine that ships could see it far out at sea.

"How strong is the light from the mantle?" she asked.

Axel started behaving like a fussy old teacher. "It's not the mantle that matters," he said. "That only gives out about six hundred candlepower—not much more than your dad's old lamp."

34

"Well, what then?"

"The lenses."

"They make it stronger—the light, I mean?"

He smiled. "Just a bit."

"How much?"

"About a hundred fifty thousand candlepower."

She sucked in her breath. "A hundred fifty thousand!"

"The lenses throw out a dazzling white beam; you can see it leagues and leagues away."

"But how does it work?"

"There are three lenses—we used to call them *bull's-eyes*—and they turn slowly so that one of them is lined up to shoot out a beam of light through the opening there every five seconds. To a ship it's just a regular flash."

It all began to dawn on her. "The light doesn't flash on and off at all?"

He laughed. "The light burns steadily all night long. Keeps going continuously from sunset to sunrise. Never stops." He was enjoying himself very much. "See, you've only been up here for a couple of minutes and you've learned something already."

She didn't mind his cheekiness. "Well, then, what makes the lenses turn?"

"Clockwork."

"Clockwork?"

"It has to be as accurate as a clock—to give a flash every five seconds. Otherwise a ship might mistake it for a different lighthouse altogether—one with a seven-second flash or a three-second flash. And that could mean a disaster, even on a calm night."

"Each one is different?"

"Each one has a code. So when a captain in this area sees a five-second light winking through the storm clouds and the rain, he breathes a big sigh and says, 'Ah, there's the good old Hammerhead Light!' And maybe he says a blessing too."

Axel took her around to the other side of the light and pointed to the frame that held the lenses. "We call all this the *optics*. It floats on a bath of mercury so that it turns smoothly and easily when it's driven by these cogs. Otherwise the lenses wouldn't move into the right place at the right time."

"And the cogs are driven by the clockwork?"

"The cogs *are* the clockwork. They're driven by those big weights you saw hanging on the end of the cable. You wind them up every few hours—with a handle."

"And that's hard work?"

"Not as hard as pumping up the air cylinder to supply pressure for the lamp. That has to be done three or four times a night with an old hand pump."

"I wouldn't like that."

"Gives you a back shaped like a big question mark."

"What other worries did you have?"

"Moths flying into the mantle were the worst of the lot. Always trying to kill themselves—and put out the light at the same time."

"Why do they do it, the silly creatures?"

"All creatures do it; even birds."

"Why?"

"They're dazzled, mesmerized. They don't know what they're doing."

Tessa looked around her. "The lightkeepers worked a

lot harder than I thought they did. Perhaps it's just as well the old lighthouses are being exchanged for automatic ones."

Axel snorted. "The old Hammerhead was the most reliable light on the coast. And it still would be if they'd let it." He pointed disgustedly at the beacon on Anvil Rock. "Just compare it with that thing down there on the Anvil. Looks like a spider with frozen legs and one eye."

"But it's automatic," said Tessa.

"Oh yes, it's automatic," Axel answered sarcastically, "until it suddenly needs to be fixed up in a big storm. Then only the albatrosses can get to it."

They were both looking out at the scene far below— the cold gray sea ribbed with angry whitecaps, the stubborn rocks of the coastline, the little village huddled at one end of the bay like a toy town, the soft folds of green land behind the coast, the flat panes of the lakes shining in the cloudy light.

"It's beautiful," said Tessa. "All of it is beautiful. Snapper Bay is a lovely, lovely place, and we're lucky to live here."

"I'm glad you think so," said Axel slowly, "because you'll have to look after it when . . ." He paused, trying to find the right words.

"When what?" she asked at last.

He smiled. "When the time comes." Then he nudged her toward the staircase. "Anyway, it's time to think about lunch. Down you go."

She led the way, tripping down the stairs quickly and lightly. At the bottom of the first spiral she stopped and looked back. He was just beginning to follow her, his body already swallowed up by the stairwell, his head framed against the circle of light above. It made his mop of white hair glow and his face shine above his great beard. Father Christmas seemed to be coming down the biggest chimney in the world.

When they reached the bottom he stood with her for a minute in the doorway. As they paused, the high rippling note of a bird's call came to them from the mud flats behind the coast. *"Ti-ti-ti-ti-ti-ti-ti,"* it went. Axel lifted his head and cocked his ear. "Listen!" They both stood motionless.

"Ti-ti-ti-ti-ti."

He turned to her, half sad, half joyful.

"It's time," he said. "The whimbrels are moving. That fellow had better hurry or he'll be too late."

Six

The winter was cruel. There were days when Tessa thought the rocky coast protecting the bay would crumble under the combers that thundered in from the sea, and then the little town would be swept inland like a bit of cockleshell. She had never seen such breakers. They hurled themselves over the rocks of the Dragon's Mouth like mad demons; they slavered and gnawed, roared and sobbed in a lather of foam and white water; they charged, shrieking, at Anvil Rock and Hammerhead Point until columns of tortured water shot up like shell bursts and the rocky outcrops were hidden in plumes of spray.

All winter long Tessa saw little of old Axel. On weekdays the school bus picked her up when the sun was rising and brought her home again when it was setting. Her mother had very strong views about girls who came in late for tea or who tried to avoid doing the dishes or who failed to do their homework. She also had something to say about girls who wanted to run around the beach in the night, looking after old men in lighthouses. So Tessa had to stay at home.

It was only on weekends that she could visit Axel. On Saturday mornings, even though the roofs might be drumming with rain or the wind bellowing like a blizzard, she would put on her father's greatcoat and plunge off around the bay to Hammerhead Point. Strangely, her mother approved of it then.

"Better see what the old fellow is up to," she would say. "Haven't seen him for a week."

Then Tessa would be in a fever lest old Axel had come down with pneumonia on Monday morning or tumbled off the ladder on Tuesday and broken his leg. She pictured him lying there on his own, day after day, waiting for someone to come. In a few minutes she would be in such a frenzy that she would snatch up the basket of cake or fruit or biscuits that her mother had been preparing and dash off even before it was ready. But when she arrived at last, panting and exhausted, he was always as sprightly as ever. The big wooden door would swing open just before she knocked, and the bright face would be peering out at her from its vast circle of white hair.

"Hullo, Tessa."

"Hullo, Uncle Axel."

And that would be that.

The winter blew itself out at last and spring came in with patches of sunshine and broken cloud. The birds began to gather again after being scattered inland by the fury of the gales, and the fishermen ventured up The Narrows for the first time since May. The days grew longer and Tessa sometimes had time to visit the lighthouse after school once more. Old Axel himself went out much more in the fine weather and he sometimes dropped into Tessa's home for a meal, whether he was invited or not.

One Sunday morning in the middle of October Tessa woke up startled. Someone was knocking at her window. At first she was going to leap out of bed and call her father, but she checked herself just in time, for a moment later a mop of white hair popped up above the sill and a hand beckoned her furiously.

"Uncle Axel!" she said, more to herself than to him. "What on earth are you doing here at this hour?"

She padded down the passage in her pajamas and opened the back door. He was there in a flash.

"What's the matter?"

"Quick. I've got a surprise." He was bubbling over with eagerness, and his eyes were as bright as gems.

"Everyone else is still in bed," she said. "It's Sunday morning."

"Never mind them," he answered impatiently, "the sleepy old lie-abouts."

"I'll have to get dressed first. I can't go running about in my pajamas."

"Hurry up, then."

As soon as she was dressed she popped her head into Jody's room to tell Jody and Bridget where she was going. Then she set off after Axel. It was a beautiful day. The morning sun had turned the tower into a column of gold against the blue sky. The white seabirds were wheeling above the headland like windblown confetti and the air was full of busy, happy sounds.

"What a lovely day," Tessa said, panting to keep up with Axel.

"So everybody is asleep in bed," he said sarcastically, "when they should be using their tongues to taste the dew on the grass."

"But it's Sunday."

"All the more reason to be thanking the Lord."

She looked at him. "You *are* excited, aren't you?"

He avoided giving her a straight answer. "You'll see," he said craftily.

They hurried across the Hammerhead Handle— cracked and battered more than ever by the winter storms—and finally reached the lighthouse door.

"Careful now," he said. "Go in slowly."

She pushed the door forward gently and peered inside. It was almost as if she had done it all before, because a big box was standing in the middle of the room. Inside it was a bird with a light stripe above each eye and a long downward-curving beak. But it only had one leg.

"Willie!" she shouted. "Willie Whimbrel!"

"Shhh!" said Axel. "Don't yell at him."

Tessa went up to the box slowly and peered at the whimbrel. "Has he lost his foot again?"

"Part of it." Axel bent down with his hands on his knees. "But it lasted a long time," he added proudly.

"How did you find him again?"

Axel straightened up. "He came looking for me, I reckon. Down in the hollow near the old shack."

42

"Did he let you catch him, then?"

"Half and half. He was a bit shy."

"Are you going to make a new foot for him?"

"Yes. You can help me. And then we'll let him run free inside the tower for a while, until he's strong again."

"Is he weak, then?"

"Pretty weak. Mostly skin and bone."

She paused. "Do you think he's just come back from the other side of the world?"

"I don't know. Maybe he has. Or maybe he had to stay in Australia."

"He would have had a bad time of it here this year."

"No worse than flying to Siberia and back."

"I guess not."

She peered closely at Willie Whimbrel and clicked her tongue.

"You poor fellow. Whichever choice you made you must have had a terrible time."

"Help me with him," said Axel, "while I take off his old foot."

Tessa held the whimbrel firmly and kindly while Axel snipped away the clamp. The plastic stem had split and the foot had turned sideways, making it impossible for Willie to walk properly or to stand upright.

"How is his other foot?" Tessa asked.

"Not bad. The claw is deformed, but otherwise it looks fine."

"What will you use for the new one?"

"Softer plastic that won't split. This time it'll last for years. Ten years, I reckon."

"Ten years!"

"Yes." He smiled. "Or at least as long as Willie lasts."

They worked together for most of the day until Axel was satisfied. Then they put the empty box outside in the stone yard and set Willie free inside the lighthouse. He fluttered and pranced on his new foot for a while, but before long he walked about quite freely, investigating everything in the room. He let them come near him to offer bits of food, so long as they moved slowly and gently. If they made a sudden movement he tended to flap away or hide on top of the cupboard.

"He's built for the mud flats and marshy plains," said Axel, "not for the inside of kitchens or lighthouses."

Before long Willie was quite tame. He would come forward to be fed and he allowed himself to be stroked gently on the back of the head. But he still disliked sudden movements.

"When are you going to set him free again?" Tessa asked one day.

"Pretty soon."

She eyed him candidly. "Don't you want to?"

He shuffled uncomfortably. "Wouldn't be right to keep him here for good."

"No."

"So he'll have to go sooner or later."

"When, then?"

"When he's fat and strong again. Another week, maybe."

Tessa knew she was being cruel. Axel had almost reached the point where he couldn't part with Willie. And neither could she.

"Are you going to take him down to the mud flats, the same as before?"

44

Axel screwed up his face as if hurt by a sudden pain. "No need for that," he said. "Might . . . might just open the door and let him make up his own mind; let him walk out if he wants to."

Tessa sat silently for a long time. "When you do," she said at last, "don't let me know about it." She swallowed a lump in her throat. "Not until it's over."

He nodded.

And a week later that was the way he did it. The next time Tessa called at the lighthouse Willie had gone.

Seven

Summer came in with school holidays and fishing. At first Tessa's mother tried to find enough jobs in the house to keep her daughter busy all day, but after a week she gave up in despair. Tessa heard her talking to her father one night. "It's like trying to keep a wild stallion tied up in the kitchen," she said. "I'd sooner let her go and have some peace."

"I'll take her out fishing," her father said. "That'll knock the steam out of her."

Tessa made three trips with Jody and her father, and two with her father and old Axel. And each time they came in with the boat loaded.

"Tessa's a lucky mascot," her father said. "And I thought she'd be a Jonah."

"It was the rough winter," said Axel, stroking his beard and looking like a prophet from the Bible. "I knew we'd reap plenty of fishes."

One day Tessa, Jody, and their father were coming

46

down The Narrows, with the Hammerhead Point loom-
ing ahead of them and the lighthouse itself towering
awesomely above it.

"Take a look at that tower," Mr. Noble said. "It's off
center, I reckon."

"It's listing," said Tessa. "It's canting off the vertical."

Her father gave her an astonished look. "Whoever
taught you to speak like that?"

"The men from Adelaide. They said it the last time
they were here."

"Did they now? And does old Axel know about it?"

"Of course he does. But he won't listen."

"Before long he may have to listen."

The next day Tessa found out what her father meant.
The government in Adelaide had decided to do something at last. There was to be a public inquiry into all the
old lighthouses along the coast to see which ones should
be kept as historic monuments. The rest would be pulled
down. A special committee of three men was to visit all
the ports and towns to see what the local people
thought. Then there would be a written report, and
finally a decision by the government. Then everyone
would know what was going to happen to the Hammerhead Light. But it would take two years.

Old Axel snorted when he heard about it. "Two
years," he jeered. "It'll take twenty-two. I'll be a hundred by the time they're finished."

Christmas came and went, and New Year's Day, and
the long hot weeks of January. Tessa's life was made up
of beach sand and saltwater, of salads for lunch and

fishing trips with her father, of long visits to Axel and short minutes at home with the broom in the kitchen. Sometimes in the evenings when the air was still she heard a high rippling whistle coming from the marshy flats and sedges behind the town: *ti-ti-ti-ti-ti-ti-ti*. She would sit quite still, then, waiting to see whether the call would be repeated.

"Willie Whimbrel," she would whisper to herself. "I wonder how you are tonight."

But no one ever answered.

Before long it was schooltime again and she was rattling along to the area school at Spoonbill Creek in the old bus that everyone called the Yellow Peril. Then it was March and autumn and her thirteenth birthday. There was a party and presents and a cake, and a loud comment from someone—"Good gracious, girl, you're growing as tall and thin as a rake."

The words startled Tessa. When everyone had gone home she shut the door of her room firmly and stood looking at herself in the mirror. It was true. She was growing so fast that before long she would be as tall as her mother. And she was ugly—bony and edgy with bumps in the wrong places and hair like mouse fur. No nice curves—only bones and points.

She considered herself carefully for a while, then poked her tongue at her own image and turned her back on it. What did it matter anyway? The longer her legs grew, the faster she could run along the beach; and the more mouselike her hair became, the less it mattered when the wind caught it and swirled it into a mess. She had to live her own life, Tessa Noble's life. Because she was Tessa Noble.

One Saturday morning a month later she got up early and went on one of her walkabouts along the coast. The sky was gray and the smell of winter was in the air. But the breeze was gentle and the waves rolled in on a long smooth swell. As she skirted the cliffs behind the Hammerhead she had a sudden thought: she would surprise Axel by hammering on his door and calling him a sleepy old lie-about. She crept quietly across the Handle and made for the door on the tips of her toes. Then she suddenly stopped. For Axel was standing with his back to her at the entrance to the little stone yard. He was bending forward, talking in low tones and stretching out his hand in a friendly gesture. Tessa took a step sideways, craning her neck to see what was going on. And then she saw. A bird with mottled feathers and a long downward-curving beak was standing in front of Axel, feeding. A bird with a stripe above the eye, and a plastic foot. Willie Whimbrel.

Axel was so intent on what he was doing that he had no idea Tessa was standing behind him. He made clicking noises with his tongue and Willie responded by coming right up to him and feeding from his hand. Then Axel leaned forward and stroked him gently on the nape of his head, making friendly little sounds all the time like a mother whimbrel talking to her baby.

Tessa almost cried and smiled at once. She had tears in her eyes for the sight of an old man and a wild creature meeting together on the high headland in the morning; tears for the trust of such a traveler who had flown high across the world through all the dangers of faraway places; tears for a man who could kneel on the hard stone as if he was saying his prayers and stretch

49

out his hand so gently that it touched the little head in front of him like thistledown. But she smiled too at the sight of a tough old fisherman leaning forward so far that his beard touched the ground; the sight of a one-time sailor who had roared on ketches and yelled above hurricanes talking baby talk like an old aunt.

At last Axel stood up slowly and moved toward the lighthouse door. The whimbrel retreated a little way across the yard, paused for a second, and then rose up and swept off across the coast. Tessa took a step forward and Axel noticed her for the first time. His face was shining.

"Hullo, Tessa girl," he said simply.

"Willie," she said. "He's so tame—and so trusting."

The old man smiled. "And trusting," he said simply. "He just comes for his breakfast."

"How long?" she asked. "How long has it been?"

"Must be all of two months now." He looked at her eagerly. "For a long time he wouldn't come any nearer than the Handle. Then he came to the yard. Now he'll come to the door if I coax him—even right inside."

She eyed him accusingly. "You didn't tell me."

He dropped his gaze and seemed embarrassed.

"I was waiting . . ." he began.

"To see if he'd stay?"

"That's about it."

There was a short silence. Tessa sensed the conflict of his feelings: a great wish that Willie Whimbrel should have his freedom, and a desperate hope that he would stay behind to brighten an old man's lonely life in a lighthouse during the winter.

50

He turned toward Tessa and took her hand. "I think he'll stay," he said excitedly. "It's late April already, and most of the whimbrels have gone. I've been watching every day. The other birds too, the migrating ones. They've been thinning out. Hardly any left now."

"But Willie's still here."

"He's still here. Some mornings he flies off to the east and I think to myself, *That's it; he's going this time.* But next morning he's back. Bless him, he's back." Axel's voice broke for a second and he pretended to have a frog in his throat. "I hope he stays," he said at last. "I hope he stays."

In a sudden flood of understanding Tessa saw something she had never fully understood before. Axel was lonely. Terribly, desperately lonely. In spite of all his hardihood, his rough life, his strength to fend for himself, he needed the trust and friendship of a little wild creature. He needed a whimbrel.

"Come inside," she said. "I'll make some tea."

They hardly spoke while she heated the water on the Primus stove and warmed the pot. They were thinking their own thoughts, and Tessa's were in a turmoil even greater than Axel's. Things were changing between them. She wasn't a little girl anymore, listening to his stories and his teachings, laughing at his yarns and teasing jokes. She was growing up. And he was growing older. Suddenly and strangely she was beginning to feel responsible for him; she was even making tea to cheer him up.

She poured two cups and handed one to him—strong and black, the way he liked it.

"He'll come back," she said quietly. "Even if he goes now, he'll be back in October."

The old man roused himself and smiled. "Of course he will," he answered, sipping noisily. "Of course he will."

But Willie Whimbrel didn't go. April turned to May, and still he came to the lighthouse every morning for his food and a torrent of trembling eager words from Axel. The days shortened and the winds grew sharp, but still he stayed. And then at last, with the bleak fury of the June storms whipping the whitecaps on the bay and flattening the marshy sedges, Axel finally coaxed his little friend inside and kept him there.

"Willie's staying with me for the winter," he told Tessa the next time she came. "Just for the worst of the rough weather."

"Bless him," Tessa said. "Bless both of you."

Willie had his own hideaway in a big crate that was open in front but pushed far back behind the other furniture so that he wouldn't be disturbed. Sometimes he came out and looked about wisely, and if suddenly startled by something unexpected he flew up hastily on top of the cupboard. But when he was alone with Axel he came out quietly and walked about like a rather superior boarder.

"Hullo Willie," Axel would say. The whimbrel would cock its head and rake the air with its big bill. "Miserable weather," Axel would add. "Can't wait for September when we can both go about our business again."

But Willie said nothing. Not even a long cry in the evening—*ti-ti-ti-ti-ti-ti-ti-ti*. It made Axel sad. Though Willie was free in a way, it suggested the silence of a

52

caged bird. And so Axel argued with himself about honesty and freedom. He was just keeping him for Willie's own good, to protect him and keep him warm through the winter, and to see that he didn't starve. As soon as the weather improved Willie could go free.

Tessa reassured him too. "Don't fret," she said. "In September you'll both be free again."

Eight

It was good that Axel had taken Willie Whimbrel indoors, for that winter was the worst on record. The storms raged ceaselessly. Twice the jetty in front of the town had its decking stripped off and once the school bus nearly upended the children of Snapper Bay into the floodwaters of Spoonbill Creek when a sudden downpour caught the driver unawares.

Two things, luckily, broke the monotony of the dreary winter days. One was a public meeting in the district hall to discuss the Hammerhead Light; the other was the new boat that Tessa's father had bought.

The meeting was one of the liveliest in years. The special committee of three men that had been set up by the government to investigate all the old lighthouses came down to listen to the local people and to give them advice. They told the meeting that it was useless trying to save the Hammerhead Light because the tower was too rickety. Some of the people hissed and booed when they heard that, and Mr. Billing, the chairman, had to cry out "Order! Order!" like someone in Parliament.

Tessa's father asked the committeemen whether they could prove that the tower was dangerous, and whether they had taken any new measurements lately. Then the men admitted that they hadn't been up there recently, and several people called out, "Why not? Why not?" Whereupon one of the men stood up angrily and said, "Because old Methuselah over there is squatting in the lighthouse and keeping everybody away with a blunderbuss as big as a cannon." And he pointed to Axel, who was sitting in the front row stroking his beard and swishing the end of it from side to side like the tail of a fidgety horse. The people stamped and laughed and cheered at that, and finally stood up and clapped for Axel, even though he hadn't said a thing.

The committee did not get very far. Even though Mr. Billing kept telling the meeting that they had to do things properly and send in official suggestions explaining why the Hammerhead Light should be saved, the people of Snapper Bay would not listen. They said that the lighthouse should stay where it was and that Axel Jorgensen should be allowed to live in it for as long as he wanted to.

In the end the committee packed up and went back to Adelaide. But they warned everyone that the final announcement would be made as soon as their report was finished. Then the tower would certainly be stripped and destroyed.

The meeting caused such a hubbub that people almost forgot about the second item of conversation in Snapper

Bay. This was Harry Noble's new boat. It was really an old ketch that had been refitted and cleaned up until it looked as smart as paint. Although it had a big diesel motor in the engine room Tessa's father had kept the sails too, just to take a few tourists out on day sailing trips when things were slack.

The whole family had to think hard to find a name for the ketch. Jody wanted it to be called *Ketchup*, Bridget wanted *Noble Boat* after the family name, and Tessa's mother thought the most honest title would be *Leaky Old Tub*. But in the end they all agreed on *Cuttlefish*, which was Tessa's suggestion, and Bridget was appointed official signwriter to paint the new name boldly on the bows and stern. Mr. Noble announced that as soon as the weather improved they would all go out on what he called a shakedown cruise to "see how the old girl behaved."

Toward the end of the winter there was another sensation. Tiny Herbert and Joe Zucci were arrested for shooting in the sanctuary. Although it was sad to see anybody arrested by the police, everyone was glad that it had happened at last. For years Tiny and Joe had been going about like maniacs, shooting at anything at all. Only a few months earlier, when Tessa had been walking along the edge of Spoonbill Lake, she had come upon a beautiful white egret shot through the breast and gasping out its life on the grassy bank. It had died in her arms, the blood from its breast feathers staining her shirt and running down her wrists in a red trickle. Shortly before, she had seen Tiny and Joe running into the thick scrub on the far shore of the lake but, although

56

she had told her father about it, there was no proof and nothing could be done.

She had cried and cried after that, not just for a dead egret, but for beauty lost forever, life cut short, loveliness destroyed; cried for cruelty and violence and stupidity and ignorance; cried for all the pain in the world, the senseless hurt, the savagery under the skin of human beings that she saw with horror and sensed with dread.

But now Tiny and Joe had been caught red-handed. They were going to be tried in the court at Mount Gambier and everybody hoped that they would be given a stiff sentence and be prevented from carrying guns for a long time.

And so the days went by and the weather slowly cleared. Tessa had seen little of Axel during the wild winter months and now, when she went to visit him, she was surprised to see him looking tired and old.

"Been a bad winter," he said simply, "enough to give a man the mopes."

"How's Willie?" Tessa asked. "Did he have a bad winter too?"

Axel brightened. "Better than he would have had out there," and he nodded toward the door. He scratched his head and chuckled softly. "We're real mates now. We have long yarns together in front of the stove and listen to the wind bellowing at us on the other side of the wall."

"How did the tower stand up to the big storms?"

"A bit creaky; getting a bit creaky, just like me."

When Tessa had a good look around outside, however,

she was appalled. The crack across the Hammerhead had widened into a great crevasse—deep and black and full of the sea's hissing and rumbling far below. All along the Hammerhead the waves had torn out chunks and fissures or gouged into the cliffs so deeply that huge masses of capping rock jutted out perilously above the chasm. In places the Hammerhead Handle had been undercut so much that it was in danger of becoming an open arch with a maelstrom rushing through the gap beneath.

But it wasn't until Tessa started to help carry some things up the steel ladder into Axel's bedroom that she really realized what was happening. She was standing at the bottom of the spiral staircase craning to look up the great tunnel of light above her, when she caught sight of the winding weights hanging on the end of the steel cable. They were different, but for a minute she could not make out why. She was about to call Axel when she saw what it was. The weights, which should have been hanging straight down exactly in the middle of the spiral, were actually hanging far to one side, almost touching the edge of the staircase. She seized a weight, pushed it out into the center, and let go. It swung back at once, clanging against the steel framework like a great gong. She had once seen Otto Kraut, the stonemason, using a plumb line on a wall, so she could read the message of the weights clearly enough. The tower was leaning. There was no doubt about it. You could even measure the distance now.

She glanced at Axel to see if he had noticed, and then looked away quickly. She had a feeling that he really knew much more than he was willing to say, or perhaps than he was willing to admit to himself.

Outside in the little yard a few minutes later they talked about Willie again, ignoring the big new cracks in the wall of the lighthouse behind them.

"As soon as the time comes," said Axel slowly, "I'll have to let Willie out."

"As soon as the weather gets warmer?"

"When the flocks return; when I hear the first *ti-ti-ti-ti-ti-ti-ti* along the creek."

"The first whimbrels back from the north."

Axel sighed. "Then he'll be free again. I've promised him that."

Nine

It was the beginning of September. Everything was peaceful and sleepy in Snapper Bay. Tessa and Axel had no idea that within a week their lives would be changed forever.

It began when Tessa's father was offered an unusual job in the *Cuttlefish*. Old Mrs. de Garis of Ibis Downs Station had bought a lot of things at a sale on Kangaroo Island and she wanted them brought back as soon as possible without all the trouble of shipping them through Adelaide—loading and unloading and loading again. So she offered to pay very well if the *Cuttlefish* could bring everything direct to Snapper Bay. Tessa's father accepted.

It was then that Jody suggested a holiday trip for everyone—a week's cruise to Kangaroo Island in the *Cuttlefish* to test the engine, shake out the sails, and bring home the bacon, as he put it. Nothing seemed more perfect. But Tessa's mother put her foot down very sternly. The school holidays had just ended, she said, and Tessa was a high-school student now; she was not going to miss her classes just to go jaunting about on pleasure cruises to Kangaroo Island.

In the end it was agreed that Tessa would stay behind and live with Mrs. Billing for a week so that she could go to school each day in the school bus. Her father and mother, Jody and Bridget, Tony Rogers from the fish factory, and young Rudy Buberic, who knew more than most people about ships and engines, were to take the *Cuttlefish* to Kangaroo Island. That was agreed. And that was how it happened.

Within two days Tessa was very lonely. She ran out of things to talk about with Mrs. Billing and she couldn't find anything interesting to read. All she could do was to mark off the days on the calendar and wait. The *Cuttlefish* left on a Sunday afternoon and it was due back at the weekend, probably on Saturday night. But that depended on the wind and the sea and the boat and the skipper's navigation and a dozen other unpredictable things.

Tessa lived through the week as doggedly as she could. At school she hid her real feelings and pretended to be happy lest some of the other girls should find out how miserable she was and call her a homesick baby. But as soon as Saturday came around she brightened up, put on her old jeans, and set off to visit Axel at the Hammerhead. She took her transistor radio and a raincoat and a bag of homemade biscuits from Mrs. Billing "as a special treat for that poor old man living all by himself up there."

As she was walking along the main street toward the jetty she heard someone calling her name, and Mrs. Humble, the postmistress, came running out with news for her. It was a telephone message saying that the *Cuttlefish* had left Kangaroo Island at six o'clock that morning and was running straight back to Snapper Bay. Tessa skipped at the news and swung the bag of biscuits around three times to celebrate. Although the *Cuttlefish* had a good radio transmitter on board there was no regular receiving watch in Snapper Bay, and so messages had to be sent to other places along the coast and relayed back by telephone. She was glad the news had come through so quickly. Now she had something definite to tell Axel.

She strode on around the beach—a thin gangling figure with swinging shoulders and bony hips. It was a foul day. Huge spirals of cloud hid the sun and a blustery wind was chopping and changing like sudden clouts about her ears. Most of the birds had gone inland; only a few sea gulls and a forlorn albatross still lined up on the shore, but they were buffeted so much that half the time their feathers were swirled about like old dusters. One by one they rose up and went swooping and tumbling through the air to find shelter.

Tessa did not really mind the day. She turned her head and lifted her face into the wind. She sniffed the salt air and the rank smell of seaweed, and listened to the breakers booming on the coast. She was comforted inwardly by the knowledge that the *Cuttlefish* was coming home, and that tomorrow they would all be sitting down together again, laughing and joking at the kitchen table—she, and her father and mother, and Jody and Bridget, and perhaps old Axel too.

Because it was a long walk to the Hammerhead she had time for other things as well—time to pick up a clean new shell, time to look at a dead crab's claw as big as a pair of tongs, time to think her own thoughts. What would she be doing in a few years' time when she was grown up? Who would pay the two-hundred-dollar fines that had been imposed on Tiny Herbert and Joe Zucci? Why did people shoot birds like that? Why were some kind and others cruel, some aggressive and others gentle? How did sea worms make their holes and why did cormorants have to hold out their wings to dry? Would the lighthouse be pulled down just because the men on the government committee were angry with the people of Snapper Bay?

She reached the rocky path that led up from the beach to the Hammerhead Handle and climbed up, locking her knees deliberately at each step in quick jerky movements. The Handle was a perilous crossing now. The waves had scoured it more than ever and there was a real danger that one day soon a sudden gust would sweep someone over the side. She crawfished her way across, leaning into the wind until she reached the wide bench of the Hammerhead, and then ran quickly to the tower door.

Axel had seen her coming and was waiting for her. "Come and look," he said, leading her around the tower to the little stone yard outside. "My old mate's back."

At first she didn't know what he meant. Then a thought struck her.

63

"Rump . . . ?" she asked, hesitatingly.

"Rump," he answered, nodding. "He got into Mrs. Snelling's garden the day before yesterday. Made a terrible mess."

"I'll bet she was cross."

"She was as wild as an adder. Wanted to shoot him on the spot, but finally brought him over to me."

"What are you going to do with him?"

The old man looked sad. "Going to send him away. Back to the reserve where he came from—near Blanchetown by the Murray River."

"How?"

"Young Thompson's taking him up. Next Monday."

They were leaning against the wall looking at Rump, who was dozing in a rough shelter made of boxes and sacks. He woke up at the sound of their voices and came trundling around the yard, whiffling and snuffling.

"Best thing," Axel said. "Too lonely for him here; no other wombats left in these parts."

The wind caught his words and swept them away. It whistled over the headland and whipped his beard against his chest. His big mop of hair streamed and thrashed about, hiding his face in such a tousle that he looked like an old English sheepdog.

"Blasted wind," he yelled. "We had better go inside."

They made their way around the tower again, escaping into the room at last and shutting the door hastily behind them.

"Madman's weather," he said. "Bad enough to turn your head."

Tessa was trying to catch her breath. "Bit wild up here," she said.

Axel looked at the ceiling as if listening for special signs from heaven. "Blow coming," he said. "I can feel it in my bones."

"A low."

"Who said a low?"

"The weather report this morning." She nodded at the radio she was still holding in her hand. "But not till tomorrow."

"Be here before tomorrow. I can tell it in my bones."

Tessa didn't argue with Axel's bones because they had often foretold storms, floods, fine weather, and big catches of fish.

"It better not come too soon," she said. "The *Cuttlefish* is on her way home."

He looked up quickly. "When?"

She told him about Mrs. Humble and the six-o'clock message. It made him uneasy.

"They should have left earlier," he said.

"How long will it take them—from Kangaroo Island?"

"Fifteen, twenty hours. Running with the sea."

"It'll be dark by then."

"Long time dark. Ten o'clock, midnight. And tonight's no night to be wallowing offshore. They'll have to bring her in."

"Well I hope they hurry."

"Amen," he said like a great bearded priest, a thousand years old.

Tessa put down her things and handed the biscuits to Axel. "For you," she said, "from Mrs. Billing." She turned and searched the room. "Where's Willie?"

Axel smiled suddenly and pointed up the ladder.

"Upstairs today," he answered, "having a look around."

"Is he getting restless?"

Axel looked a little downcast. "Maybe." He hesitated a little. "I was planning to let him go this weekend. But not in such weather."

"Are any of the whimbrels back?"

"Haven't seen any yet. Been watching each day— with the telescope."

There was another pause.

"Shouldn't be long, though," she suggested.

"Shouldn't be long. A week maybe."

He looked away as if in sudden pain.

"I'll just leave the door open. Let him walk out."

"That's the best way."

"By far the best way, I reckon."

She looked around the crowded room, at the jumble of odds and ends, the mess of unwashed pots and cups.

"I'll tidy up a bit," she said. "I'll do the dishes and make the bed."

"It could do with a bit of a cleanup." He looked at the ceiling again. "Be careful upstairs, though. Move sort of slowly." He smiled. "On account of someone."

She smiled back. "I'll be very careful, Uncle Axel."

The day went slowly. They had lunch and listened to the midday news on the radio. There was an intense low in the Great Australian Bight, the weather forecaster said, and it was still deepening. There would be gales in the gulfs before long.

"Wind!" said Axel angrily. "Always blowing. That's all it's good for."

Tessa laughed. "That's all it is."

66

At four o'clock they both went up to the top of the tower to look around. Axel took down the curtains and peered hard with his telescope. But there was nothing to be seen all around the horizon except a heaving wilderness of water.

"Real yeaster," he said. "All whips and whitecaps."

"No boats?"

"Not a sniff." He scanned the west again, moving the telescope slowly from right to left. "Too early for any sign of your father." He lowered the telescope slowly and folded it up. "All the same, I wish he and that old *Cockleshell* would hurry up and get back."

"*Cuttlefish,*" Tessa corrected him.

"*Cocklefish* or whatever. I'd still feel a lot happier if we could see him coming safely down The Narrows."

She looked at the breakers far below and the wind-whipped sea beyond. "I wish they'd hurry too," she said, turning away quickly and starting down the staircase. "I hate waiting."

Axel had a word with Willie Whimbrel on the way down and talked him into joining them in the bottom room again. They got the stove going and sat sipping cups of tea while Willie made an inspection of the place to see what changes Tessa had made. Then he went back into his box behind the table.

Axel watched him fondly. "People wouldn't believe it," he said suddenly, "if we said we had a whimbrel."

"A tame whimbrel?"

"They just wouldn't believe it."

"Because he's a shy fellow?"

"A rover. Wild and fast and free."

67

"It's you, Uncle Axel. No one else could have done it."

A tremendous gust of wind struck the tower and the breakers boomed below. A strange shudder, like a distant earthquake, seemed to run through the floor. The ceiling creaked. Tessa looked up quickly and then glanced questioningly at Axel.

"Blasted wind," he said. "Makes the sea mad. Even worries the old tower."

They settled down again but they were both uneasy. They knew that a great storm was coming. And the *Cuttlefish* was still a long way from home.

Ten

At five o'clock Tessa said she had to go. She put on her raincoat, said good-bye to Axel, and slipped out the door. There was a strange light outside, a kind of gloomy glow. She paused to let her eyes get used to it, then set off across the Handle, leaning against the wind so as not to be taken unawares.

She had reached the far side and was about to descend to the beach when she heard a sharp crack, like a rifle shot. It was gone in an instant, whipped away by the wind. She stopped to listen for a minute and was about to move on when she heard another one, and then another. Puzzled, she moved forward a few paces onto a small rocky hump that gave her a good view of the coast below the Hammerhead. There she stood quite still, gazing in astonishment.

Two young men with rifles were firing at something. At first she wondered what on earth it could be. There were no birds in sight anywhere, and the water was too broken for them to be firing at seals or porpoises. One of the shooters was a tall young man in a cap, the other a big fat fellow with a floppy hat pulled down over his ears. She recognized them instantly: Tiny Herbert in the cap and Joe Zucci in the hat, still and forever playing with rifles.

She stood watching as they fired again. She followed the direction of their aim and saw with a start what they were shooting at. It was the beacon on Anvil Rock.

"Hey!" she yelled. "Don't do that!" But her voice was lost on the wind. Still they fired. Ten shots, a dozen, a whole fusillade. She wondered what in the world was making them do such a thing: thrills, jokes, stupidity, or perhaps revenge for their recent fines.

"Stop that!" she yelled. "You'll smash the beacon."

Her shout must have carried down to them this time, for they looked up hastily, saw her standing aggressively on the knoll above them, and reacted guiltily. Clutching their rifles they turned and ran down the coast. Shortly afterward she saw a car lurch away from nearby Petrel Inlet and head back toward the main road.

Tessa was undecided, wondering whether to go on or not. In the end she thought it better to run back to tell Axel what she had seen.

"Hooligans," he said as soon as she had told him. "They ought to be locked up."

"Is there anything we can do?"

"About them, yes—tell the police. About the beacon, no—nothing but wait."

"What if it's broken, ruined?"

All kinds of terrible thoughts seemed suddenly to

crowd into Axel's mind. "Tessa girl," he said urgently, "can you run all the way to Snapper Bay, and all the way back?"

"I can try."

"Go to Mrs. Humble's, then. First see if there are any more messages from your father's boat. Then ask her to ring Percy Murray on Porpoise Point; he can see the Anvil Beacon from there. Ask him if it's working."

He hurried with her to the door. "Can you do that?"

"Yes."

"Good girl."

"It might take me half an hour or more."

"Just be as quick as you can. Oh, and you'd better tell Mrs. Billing what you are doing."

Tessa had made the long run around the beach many times before, but never like this—with the wind rising and the gloom gathering and a ship in peril with all her family on board. She raced over the sand. Sometimes, if she misjudged the firm damp edge or if the wind unexpectedly drove the sea far up the beach, her foot suddenly slapped down hard in the shallows and the cold water splashed up against her legs like ice. Sometimes there were sudden lulls or gusts that made her veer crazily in her tracks. But she barely noticed these things. With heart pounding and breath gasping she entered the main street at last and ran up to Mrs. Humble's door. It took only a few minutes to get answers to both of Axel's questions: according to the most recent message the *Cuttlefish* was definitely running for Snapper Bay; Percy Murray reported that the Anvil Rock beacon was dead.

Tessa didn't wait any longer. She thanked Mrs. Humble, made a hurried call on Mrs. Billing, and then set off on the long run back to the Hammerhead. She had a head wind this time. The gloom was deeper, the clouds more ominous. And she was almost exhausted. But she slogged her way around the bay again, her face stung by the wind-whipped sand, her legs numb. And so at last she stumbled dangerously across the spray-wet rocks of the Hammerhead Handle to Axel's door. There she gasped out her news, already picturing a boat trying to enter The Narrows in darkness and storm without a lifesaving beacon to mark the way.

"What are we going to do?" she asked fearfully. "They *must* see a light."

Old Axel sat hunched and silent.

"Could we tell them to go back?" she pleaded.

He shook his big tousled head. "Too late," he said, "especially with a big storm coming."

"A lamp on the headland, then? We've got a kerosene lantern."

"It would be doused in a second—snuffed out by the wind and the spray."

"We could shelter it."

"Wouldn't work. They wouldn't see it anyway."

"On the Point they might."

He shook his head again. "A few candlepower! Hopeless. They'd be onto the rocks before they got a glimpse of it."

"Two lamps, then; lots of lamps. I could run back and get some from the town."

He sat there shaking his head. "Need far more than

72

that, especially on a night like this. Need a great beam like a searchlight."

"Needs a lighthouse," she said tonelessly.

He nodded. "Yes, a lighthouse."

Suddenly she seemed to tremble a little as if she'd had an attack of fever. "A lighthouse," she repeated in a whisper. She turned to him, her face bright and her eyes shining. "Needs a lighthouse!" she cried, jumping to her feet and seizing him by the arm. "And here we are sitting underneath one. The best and biggest lighthouse on the coast."

He stood up slowly, his mouth opening in amazement. "Yes, Tessa."

"The Hammerhead," she said.

"The Hammer-blessed-Head! You can see its light halfway to Antarctica."

She was waiting for him to act, hardly daring to hope. "Can you get it going, do you think?"

"Worked here for years."

"How long will it take?"

"With the two of us—not long."

They clambered up quickly into the next room where Axel grabbed a lantern, a box of matches, and some rags. Then up the spiral they went to the floor above, where he seized a big can of kerosene and a small one of methyl alcohol.

"First job, Tessa girl," he said, panting from the fast climb up the staircase. "Fuel supply."

There were two cylinders fixed side by side near the central column of the lighthouse. Axel unscrewed the cap from one of them and together they poured in the kerosene, using an old funnel. The can was heavy and they spilled some in their haste.

"Never do, this spilling business," Axel said. "Too dangerous; in the old days we'd be hauled over the coals for sure."

When they had poured in about five gallons they screwed on the cap and put aside the empty drum.

"Second job, Tessa girl," said Axel rather breathlessly. "Start pumping."

There was a hand pump beside the second cylinder, and Axel seized it, giving a few quick pushes on the plunger. "Good, it still works."

He left her alone with the pump while he hurried up to prepare the light. "Pump as long as you can," he called back, "and then stop. At the moment we need just enough pressure to get a start."

It was dreadful work. After a few minutes her arms felt like lead and the pump handle weighed a ton. Then her back started to ache and the pain spread like a hot stain right across her shoulders. Perspiration stood out on her forehead and the drops began to join and trickle down into her eyes. She was surprised at the way they stung. But still she worked on. If her family's safety depended on the light, and the light depended on pressure, then she would see that there was plenty of it.

"That'll do," Axel called at last. "We can finish pumping later. You can come up and help here now."

She could have cried with relief. "Coming," she called, as soon as she had gathered enough breath to speak.

74

He had opened one of the bull's-eyes, taken out the burner, and cleaned it thoroughly. As she joined him he was replacing it and fitting a new mantle.

"Just as well they left everything behind when they closed down the lighthouse," he said.

"Do you think it'll work?" she asked, twisting her fingers.

"It'll work." It almost sounded as if he was gritting his teeth as he said it.

He stepped back, picked up the can of methyl alcohol, and filled the preheating dish below the burner. Then he struck a match and watched for a while as the blue flames swayed and danced.

"Now," he said. "Third job while we're waiting."

She looked at him cannily. "Not more pumping?"

"Winding."

"Oh no!"

"I'll give you a hand."

So they turned the big handle together, slowly winding up the weights from the bottom of the shaft.

"How often do we have to do this?" she asked after a while.

"Every two hours."

"It's torture," she said. "Gives you needles in your back and blisters on your hands."

"It's good for you. Builds your muscles."

Standing there side by side with their hands together on the handle in the half dark, Tessa was aware more clearly than ever of his strength and patience and skill. And his knowledge of so many things. He was a clever, kindly man, a great man.

"Reminds me of winding up the capstan," he said. "Did plenty of that in my time."

"Were you a sailor for long?"

"Twenty years. Sailor, donkey man, stoker, fireman, deckhand, cook."

"Scientist, teacher, lighthouse keeper."

"And a hippy in a hut." He chuckled at that picture of himself and whistled three bars of an old sea chanty as he wound up the weights.

"Nearly time," he said after three or four minutes. "The burner should be hot enough."

He made a long taper from a piece of rolled-up newspaper, lit one end of it, and held it above the mantle.

Tessa watched breathlessly. "It's not working," she said with sudden disappointment.

"Half a minute, half a minute," he said. "Wait till I open the valve."

He turned on a small tap in a metal pipe on the side of the frame. There was a sharp hiss and the next moment the mantle ignited in a brilliant white glow.

"Presto," he cried delightedly.

"It works," said Tessa, hugging him. "It works. It works."

He extinguished the taper and put it aside. "Not too fast," he said. "The last test is still to come."

"What's that?"

"The optics. To see if they turn."

"Of course."

"No use if they don't."

He swung the bull's-eye shut like a solid glass door and clipped it into place. Then he let the whole frame

76

ride free. It started to turn at once in a slow deliberate circle that seemed as steady and certain as the movement of the earth.

Axel grinned so broadly that his whole face glowed through his beard. "Fifteen seconds for a full turn," he said; "three bull's-eyes in the system, a five-second gap between signals." His grin widened still more. "The Hammerhead Light is shining again. I hope it strikes sparks off those fellows in Adelaide."

She laughed with relief. "And lights a track for the *Cuttlefish* all the way back into Snapper Bay."

"The five-second flash."

"The five-second flash of the Hammerhead Light."

Eleven

By the time they had pumped up the air cylinder to full pressure and wound the weights to the top of the tower it was almost seven o'clock. Then they both stood watching. Axel refused to leave because the mantle had bucked and fluttered once or twice at the beginning and he was afraid that a bit of grit might suddenly block the jet and plunge everything into darkness.

And so they waited and talked. Seven o'clock went by, half past seven, eight o'clock. The light was burning beautifully—bright, incandescent, clear. Axel stretched and yawned. "Just like old times," he said. "Only thing missing is the head lightkeeper to keep us on our toes."

"Shall I get you something to eat or drink?" Tessa asked.

"Hardly worth bothering."

"No trouble."

"A couple of biscuits, then. That'll do till the boat comes in."

She skipped down the staircase to the first floor and swung herself from the iron ladder to the ground level, where she found a lantern, lit it, and put it on a hook.

"Hullo, Willie," she called. "It's only me."

The whimbrel looked at her with sharp, bright eyes and retreated toward his box. She gathered up the bag of biscuits, two apples, and her radio, and went clambering back up to Axel again.

As she was about to put her foot on the first step of the spiral staircase a shudder like the one she had noticed earlier passed through the tower and a piece of metal clanged above her head like a broken bell. She jumped back, looking upward quickly, afraid that something was about to fall on her head. But it was only the clockwork weights. They were halfway down again now, swinging and jangling like a jolted pendulum instead of hanging straight and still as good weights should. She could hear the wind outside and feel the power of the sea. And she was afraid. If the sea could send tremors through hills of solid rock, what could it do to a little ketch that was as weak as a walnut shell.

She shuddered. But then, when she looked up the high tunnel of the staircase toward the pinnacle above her, she was hopeful too. For up there the lenses were slowly turning—silent, unfaltering, dependable—hurling out their great beam like a solid bolt of light. Over the yeasty whitecaps, over the spume and spindrift, high above rocks and the tortured storm-wracked breakers, the Hammerhead Light was flinging out its light again like a challenge. As it had done for a hundred years.

Tessa stood where she was, one hand on the spiral

handrail, her face turned upward as if listening to a far message—the voices of a million voyagers in the dark. Even now, perhaps, her father was adding the final shout: "It's the Hammerhead, Jody, the Hammerhead Light. The five-second flash of the Hammerhead Light."

A tremendous wave struck the cliffs and the handrail shivered in Tessa's palm. The whole tower creaked. She roused herself and climbed quickly back to Axel.

He was standing in front of the thick glass panels peering into the darkness. He hadn't heard her coming. Again, as she looked at him, she felt proud and grateful that he was her friend: the broad back still seemed so young, the big shoulders so strong, the huge shock of hair so fiercely independent.

"Come on," she heard him say under his breath. "Come on, come on."

She moved up beside him, offering apples and biscuits.

"What's the time, Tessa?" he asked.

"Nearly half past eight."

"Should soon be time." He paused. "*Must* soon be time."

She was heartened and frightened, all at the same time. "As early as this?" she asked.

He paced from pane to pane, munching and peering. "With the wind behind them they should be traveling like a speedboat, *Cockleshell* or no *Cockleshell*."

"*Cuttlefish*," she corrected.

"*Coddlefish*," he said wryly.

Nine o'clock came. They pumped up the air cylinder again and wound up the weights. Half past nine . . . ten o'clock. Still there was no sign.

They were both very tense now. Tessa was close to tears, but she held them back sternly so as not to disgrace herself in front of him. They both listened to the ten-o'clock news and the weather report, and then she hastily switched off the radio. The gales were already causing havoc in the gulfs, the reporter said, and the storm front was moving rapidly eastward.

"What are they doing?" Axel blurted out impatiently. "What on earth are they doing?"

Another half hour went by. Tessa was very frightened now. She felt that she was trapped and helpless in the center of giant forces of terrible power and violence. So were her father and mother, and Jody and Bridget, and there was nothing anyone could do.

"Perhaps they've turned back after all," she said at last. Her voice was thin and unconvincing.

"Couldn't," he answered tersely. "Madness to head into a storm like that."

"Then perhaps they've run for shelter somewhere?"

"There isn't any shelter. It's Snapper Bay or nothing."

They were silent again.

"We would . . . we could see their lights, couldn't we, Uncle Axel?" she asked timidly.

"Should see their masthead lights, even in this mash—unless they've had the stuffing knocked out of them."

She had no way of knowing what he was really thinking now—whether he was starting to give up, admitting to himself that the *Cuttlefish* was already at the bottom of the sea. She told herself that she wouldn't give up,

81

not ever: she would go on hoping to midnight, to day-break, to midday tomorrow if she had to.

"There!"

Axel almost sprang at the glass, pouncing forward, jabbing with his stubby finger.

"Where? Where?"

"Still well out. . . . See the red lights?"

She missed them at first, but then she saw them winking and dipping like tiny pinpricks. "Yes, yes, I see them, I see them." She cried then, just a bit, and tried to pretend that she was laughing, to cover up the tremors in her voice. "Yes, I can see them now."

Axel had his nose right against the pane. "They're coming in," he said. "Easy, easy." He was talking to Tessa and to the ship, and to himself, all at once. "Keep her leeward, keep her bow leeward," he told the pane of glass breathlessly. "Watch out for the Anvil! Keep to starboard, away from the Anvil!"

The *Cuttlefish* was starting her life-and-death run for The Narrows. It was like an ant trying to swim into a crack on the side of a whirlpool. She had to come in between Anvil Rock on one side and the Dragon's Mouth on the other, a passage less than eighty yards wide. And there was only one chance; if she missed the opening on her first run there was no going back for a second try. She would be smashed to pieces in a minute.

The worst part of the agony was now starting for Tessa because she could actually see the little ship fighting for its life.

"It's up to your father now—to find the mouth of The

Narrows." He looked at her reassuringly. "No one knows it better than he does."

She was peering tensely at the little winking lights. Sometimes they disappeared completely as if snuffed out by a giant wave; then suddenly they winked on again, brightly and bravely in the darkness.

"He knows that entrance, your dad does. So does Jody."

The lights seemed to take a long time to make any headway, but Axel told her not to worry. "Hard to judge it when a boat's coming straight in; seems to be standing still." He changed his position and peered again. "They're moving all right; coming in fast."

"How long?" she asked breathlessly.

"Ten minutes. Fifteen, maybe."

They both watched tensely. "It's not raining yet, thank God," he said after a while. "Ruins visibility in a small boat."

"Yes," she answered mechanically, fearing that the downpour would start at any minute.

"The Dragon's Mouth is clear enough. Breakers everywhere. White water. He'll see that."

"Yes."

"The Rock's the secret. The Anvil. He has to come close in under." He paused again. "Not too close, though."

"Will it stand out enough—the shape in the dark?"

"He should pick it up. As long as the rain holds off."

"It will. I know it will."

"As long as he keeps his bearings, a landmark or two in the dark." He turned to her. "Tell you what. Put a few lanterns in the windows. Show up the tower a bit."

She ran to get them. "There's one hanging on the wall above the bed," he called, "and another one down in the kitchen. There's a flashlight somewhere, too."

She raced down the staircase and swung herself from the ladder in one leap.

She found the flashlight and was about to seize the lantern from its hook when she had a sudden urge to look outside. Watching the *Cuttlefish* through the thick glass of the lighthouse windows had been like looking into a fishbowl. She wanted to see it in the open air.

She went to the door, swung it open, and ran outside. The night was so dark that she had to stop for a minute to get her bearings. No moon, no stars, no lights; only a strange lull in the wind. She ran around the tower, using the flashlight, and peered earnestly out to sea. There were the lights of the *Cuttlefish*, not even winking anymore but riding clear and free, coming up to the mouth of The Narrows.

Tessa turned and ran back inside. As she did so her foot caught on something near the doorway and she fell sprawling against the table, sending everything down with a shattering crash. At the same time there was a startled flutter behind her, then the sound of flapping wings. She raised herself quickly on one elbow and just caught a glimpse of a shape flying through the open doorway. It seemed to be held there for an instant in the outline of the opening before swerving off into the darkness.

"Willie!" she cried. "Oh, Willie!"

But Willie had gone. Startled by the din of her falling

84

and the crash of the table against his box, confused by his sudden plunge into the dark, he was flying wildly outside somewhere between heaven and earth.

Tessa was so distraught that she forgot all about the lanterns.

"Uncle Axel!" she cried out, clambering desperately up the ladder. "Uncle Axel! Willie's flown away." She reached the first landing and tumbled blindly up the staircase, calling as she went.

At the same time he gave a great shout that echoed down to her. "They're through! They're through the entrance." He had been watching the *Cuttlefish* so intently that he hadn't heard a word she had said.

She was still only halfway up the spiral. "Uncle Axel," she kept repeating, "Willie's flown away."

This time he heard her. He turned quickly toward the well of the staircase. "The door! Did you open it?"

Just at that moment there was a thump on the glass outside, a sharp bump like a thick mop being flung hard against it. He looked back, startled. Something was lying on the ledge outside. A shape, a bundle. He could see it through the glass near the edge of the catwalk—the precarious platform that circled the top of the tower. He peered at it hard with a strange look on his face—puzzled or stunned, it was hard to tell. Then he moved back the catch that opened the heavy pane, reached out as far as he could with his arm, and lifted the bundle inside. It was the body of Willie Whimbrel.

Tessa came rushing up the last turn of the spiral. She was torn between two desperate events. "Are they through The Narrows, are they really through?" And in the same breath, "I'm sorry, Uncle Axel. I shouldn't have opened the door."

He was kneeling with his back to her. There was something lying on the floor in front of him.

"Uncle Axel! What's the matter? Whatever's the m . . . ?"

He did not look up. Instead he lifted Willie's body in his big wrinkled hand and held it there gently, motionless and silent. Willie seemed to give a shudder and his beak opened just a fraction. Then his eyes glazed and his lower eyelids rose like little gray blinds to shut out his sharp bright gaze forever.

Willie was dead.

"Willie!" Tessa cried out. "Willie! Willie!"

She flung herself down beside him, both of them on the floor there on their knees, the wind suddenly shrieking and gusting again outside, the breakers thundering.

"Oh, Willie."

He reached out his big hand and stroked the fine head just once, the smooth feathers above the striking white stripe. But the head was lifeless now, lolling over the end of his other hand like a rag doll. Tessa drew back, horrified. And then, for the first time, she looked at Axel. His face was wrenched by an expression of suffering, like someone in great pain. And as he turned toward her a large tear that was trembling on his eyelash spilled over and ran slowly down his hairy cheek.

Tessa was stricken. She had never seen a man cry before, least of all a man like this who had spent so much of his life struggling in the rough wildernesses of the world. But she saw what it meant. It was the cry of a

86

man for the death of something in his heart, for a magical bond that was broken, for the spirit of a special creature that was born to high flight and the wide freedom of the earth, now nothing more than a lifeless bundle like an old shirt.

"Oh, Uncle Axel, what have I done?"

He brushed the back of his hand across his face.

"It was the light," he said in a thin broken voice. "It was too magic and terrible for him."

"It was so dark outside."

"He flew into it." Axel brushed his other cheek slowly like someone in a daze. "He flew into it. Just like a big moth." His voice broke completely for an instant. "He couldn't help it. He was blinded. Poor big moth."

After a minute he got to his feet, carrying Willie's body in both hands, and made for the staircase. There he sighed and seemed to take a big breath. Almost at once he was himself again.

"Time we went downstairs. Not much more to do up here."

"What about the light?"

"I'll keep it going. There might be other ships out there tonight."

They descended silently. When they were down in the big room again he put Willie's body in its box without a word. He looked at it for a few moments and then straightened up.

"They're in the bay now," he said quietly, "as safe as salmon."

She felt uneasy. "I guess I'd better go."

"Storm's almost here."

"I'll run."

"Take my flashlight then."

She put on her raincoat and stood buttoning it up at the door. He watched her.

"Good night, Uncle Axel."

"Good night, Tessa. Be careful on the Handle."

But instead of going out through the door she suddenly turned and flung herself against his shoulder.

"Oh, Uncle Axel," she sobbed, "I'm sorry, I'm sorry, I'm sorry."

He held her like a father, like a grandfather. "It's finished, Tessa. It has happened, and now it's finished. Let it be."

"But I caused it. It would never have happened if it hadn't been for me."

"Don't blame yourself, Tessa girl."

"But I do. I do, I do, I do."

She sobbed so uncontrollably that for a long time he could do nothing. At last he drew her away and led her to the door. "You must go home," he said, "or it will be too late."

She recovered herself a little, sniffling and feeling in her pockets for a handkerchief or tissue. "Sorry, Uncle Axel," she sobbed. "Sorry for me and everything I've done."

"Good night, Tessa girl."

He opened the door and led her out into the night.

"Mind the spray on the Handle; use the flashlight."

She got across just in time. The storm broke as she reached the beach, the wind shrieking like a million banshees and the rain lashing her like hail. Within seconds she was drenched in spite of the raincoat, her shoes sodden and her hair streaming.

But she hardly noticed it all. Even the sight of the *Cuttlefish*'s lights at the jetty barely roused her. For her mind was back inside the tower of the Hammerhead Light, seeing again the tears in the eyes of a white-bearded old man kneeling over the body of a whimbrel.

Twelve

Tessa arrived home at the same time as the travelers. In spite of the sadness in her heart and the utter exhaustion of her body, it was a glad, thankful reunion. They all stood in the kitchen, bedraggled and as sodden as kelp, laughing and crying at the mess they were in, at seeing each other again, at their deliverance from danger and death. Even Tessa's mother was so moved that for the first time in years she cried over Tessa and kissed her five times without pausing.

"It was the Hammerhead," her father kept repeating. "The wonderful old Hammerhead. We couldn't believe our eyes."

"The first sight of her gave us the creeps," said Jody. "We were looking for the Anvil Beacon. We thought we were seeing a ghost when we first saw the five-second flash."

"But she saved us. She saved us all right."

"Nobody's going to pull her down now," said Jody.

"The old tower will remain as a monument forever."

"Whose was the brilliant idea?" asked Mr. Noble. "And how on earth did you get her going?"

"Well, I thought of it," said Tessa. "But Uncle Axel did everything."

They finally stumbled into bed at one o'clock in the morning after the joy of warm baths, dry towels, soft pajamas, and hot cups of cocoa. Tessa fell into a deep sleep almost at once. Outside, the storm roared and shrieked over Snapper Bay, but even Tessa's father— exhausted from the struggle and agony of his voyage— barely heard it. And so, while the walls of the house stood and the roof stayed on, they slept.

Shortly before seven o'clock the next morning Tessa stirred and opened one eye. She had been vaguely aware of the fury outside and she guessed that the wind had been bellowing all night. But now it seemed to have dropped and the rain had eased. Remembering her father's bedtime joke that the Grand Hotel might move to Spoonbill Swamp during the night, she crawled out of bed and padded over to the window in her pajamas. The rest of the house was as quiet as a mousehole. Everyone else was asleep.

Tessa lifted a corner of the window shade and looked out. Two pines were down near the foreshore and a mess of cans, branches, bits of timber, and other debris littered the street. But the buildings of Snapper Bay still stood. They had been built in the old days, with thick stone walls and heavy timbers, and they had weathered many a storm before this. She was about to tiptoe back to bed when her gaze swept the bay. There were still

91

whitecaps on the water and she could see booming plumes of spray shooting up like explosions from the rocks of the Dragon's Mouth beyond the coast. It was going to be a dreadful day even though the worst of the storm had passed.

She moved back a step or two from the window, then paused and went back to look again. A moment later her shouts were waking the house.

"Dad! Dad, come quick!"

Her father came grumbling hastily along the passage.

"Look! Look at the Hammerhead!" she yelled impatiently.

Jody also hurried up in his pajamas, and so did her mother, but not Bridget. Tessa pulled the shade so violently that it shot up and flapped noisily around the roller.

"Look at the Hammerhead."

Mr. Noble took a quick look and stood quite still in disbelief. "Good grief!" he said.

The tower was jutting from the headland like a leaning post. Not just a gentle skewing, a slight shift from the vertical, but a lean like a lunatic Tower of Pisa. From Tessa's window it looked as if the top of the column, with its lightroom where she and Axel had been standing the night before, was leaning out beyond the edge of the cliff, over the channel of The Narrows like a boat's crow's nest at the top of a leaning mast.

"It's going to go," said Mr. Noble in a low voice. "It can't stand like that."

He ran back into his room, calling to Jody as he went.

92

"Get the Land Rover. And hurry."

"I'm coming too," said Tessa.

They shouted to one another in a three-way conversation while they dressed.

"Old Axel might still be in there."

"Not with a lean like that. You'd have to be out of your mind."

"Poor old Hammerhead."

"Just lasted long enough to save our bacon; not even a day to spare."

Tessa was in a fever of haste. "Hurry up," she kept calling. "He could be in very great danger."

"And so might you," said her mother. "For heaven's sake be careful."

They ran out, all three of them, and jumped into the old Land Rover. It took a minute or two of grinding and stuttering before they moved off, but at last they swung out into the street and raced off down the beach.

"Good Lord! Just look at it," said Jody.

Low clouds and scud were sweeping the Hammerhead, but now and again the murk lifted and then the tower stood out crazily like a huge uprooted pillar leaning against the clouds.

"Impossible," said Tessa's father. "It has to go."

"The whole bluff must be shifting," Jody said, "undermined by the storm."

Tessa was searching the cliffs and beaches as they sped along.

"Where's Uncle Axel?" she kept asking fearfully. "Wherever can he be?"

"We'll know in a minute."

Jody swung the Land Rover around at the end of the beach near the wreckage of the shack. Then all three ran up the rocky track that led to the Hammerhead Handle. As they reached the top of the cliffs they were searching the rocks and the leaning tower for signs of movement.

Suddenly Jody yelled at the top of his voice: "Look out! Look out ahead!"

"Stop!" Tessa's father thrust out his hands and grabbed them both. "Back! Back!"

The Handle was shattered. A gap four yards wide had been smashed right through it. The Head was now an island.

"Careful," he said. "This whole slab of rock might be undermined."

They edged their way forward until they could look down into the abyss. The sea had gouged out a narrow canyon separating the Head from the mainland, and the waves were thundering through it into the waters of Snapper Bay.

"Look at the bluff too," Jody said, pointing beyond the leaning tower. "It's been cut to pieces."

It was true. The great buttresses of rock that had protected Hammerhead Point against the sea for a thousand years had at last gone down, and a whole section of the bluff had split off along the crack that Tessa had seen. Now the waves were booming against the last remnants of the old shield and undercutting the Head itself. All that remained was a fractured island, and even that was tilting slowly, taking the tower with it.

But though the awful power of the sea was all about them, Tessa looked only at the tower.

"Uncle Axel," she screamed at the top of her voice. "Uncle Axel, are you there?"

Her father stood beside her. "He couldn't hear you, Tessa. Not if you had a voice like a foghorn."

She turned to him desperately. "He must be in there. He couldn't have got away during the night."

"Not once the bridge went down."

"He's probably sheltering inside. What else could he do? We'd do the same."

"Not me," said Jody. "Not with that monstrous tombstone leaning over me. I'd sooner sit out in the cold."

Mr. Noble turned to Jody. "Tell you what. Can you throw a stone as far as the tower?"

"I can try."

"See if you can hit the door. A solid thump ought to bring him out."

"If he's still inside."

"He's in there," Tessa said. "I know he is."

Jody searched about for four or five nuggety stones as big as tennis balls to hurl across the gap at the tower door. He was just moving up for the first throw when the door opened and Axel came out slowly. His white hair and beard streamed in the wind.

All three of them waved and cooeed but he didn't notice them. He was carrying something in his right hand. Tessa saw what it was and felt a great pang of pity. She put out her hands to silence the other two and they all stood watching. Axel walked out toward the steep cliff's edge and stood there for a minute on the verge of the precipice, with the wind thrashing his shirt. Then he lifted his hand in an underarm movement and gently threw something over the cliff. For a brief instant it was a dark spot in the air above the chasm, like a bird just taking flight; then it was caught by the wind and sent plummeting away out of sight.

"What on earth is he doing?" asked Tessa's father. "The storm must have turned his head."

"He was doing something special," Tessa said softly.

Jody looked at her strangely. "Oh. What?"

"He was burying something in the sea."

On his way back Axel noticed them for the first time. He waved and came over quickly to the edge of the gap.

"Can't get across," he yelled unnecessarily. "Can't jump the gap."

"I can see that," Mr. Noble yelled back. "You'd need to be a grasshopper or a springbok to do that."

He turned urgently to Jody. "Quick, drive back to the house and get the extension ladder from the back yard."

Jody was racing off before he had finished speaking. "And a lot of rope," Mr. Noble shouted after him, "just in case."

"I'd better get my coat," yelled Axel, "and a few things."

"I wouldn't go back in there," called Tessa's father. "I reckon she'll go with the next big wave." But Axel didn't seem worried. He disappeared through the open door again and they caught glimpses of him moving about inside, gathering up a few of his belongings as calmly as if he'd been packing for a picnic.

The tower was a fearsome sight now. It leaned grotesquely over the cliffs like some cartoonist's joke about bad builders. There were enormous cracks in the thick lower walls, some of them running up in jagged spirals around the upper sections like black fissures. Whenever a bigger wave than usual thundered against the bluff the whole column groaned like a living thing, as if wrenched by pain beyond description. Sometimes they heard wood splintering or metal clanging inside as if the tower was ringing wild bells to toll out its own doom.

Jody was back within ten minutes with the ladder lashed to the roof of the Land Rover, making it look like a boastful little fire engine. Other people in the town had noticed the tower by now and dozens of them were streaming around the beach, jostling and pointing. The first of them helped Jody up the rocks with the ladder.

"Come on, Axel," Tessa's father bellowed through his cupped hands. He turned to Jody and a couple of other men who were lending a hand. "Separate the two sections of the ladder," he said, "and lash them together side by side. Then tie a rope to one end and hoist them upright."

They managed to get the ladders standing vertically after a lot of grunting and shuffling and a good many cries of alarm and advice. Then they lowered the high end slowly across the gap with the rope, like a drawbridge. The ladders reached across nicely, with a bit to spare.

"What a bridge," said Jody. "Who's going to walk the plank?"

"I suppose I'll have to," said his father. "Just see that you anchor this end as solid as a rock."

"That's not too solid," Jody answered, "not around here."

97

Mr. Noble crawled slowly onto the ladders, hand over hand.

"Don't look down! Don't look down!" called several of the watchers.

He didn't answer or look back, but gazed steadily ahead at the opposite bank. In a few moments he was across and standing up on the other side. People clapped and cheered.

"Come on, Axel," he called, running toward the tower. "Let's get you out of here."

Axel emerged through the doorway carrying his coat and a couple of bundles. Tessa watched spellbound. It all seemed so sad. Axel was being forced out of the tower at last, not by committees or laws or men from Adelaide, but by violent powers that were stronger than any man. He suddenly looked old and small in the shadow of the huge leaning pillar behind him, a white-headed old man of seventy-three, carrying all he owned in the world— a coat and two small bundles. She felt a great pity for him, for all that he had suffered. And now he had this last terrifying bridge to cross.

"Uncle Axel," she said under her breath. "Be careful, Uncle Axel."

"We can't both cross at once," she heard her father shout. "The ladders wouldn't take the weight." He turned to Axel. "You'd better go first. Do you think you can manage it?"

Axel moved forward toward the edge of the gap. Suddenly he paused, dropped the things he was carrying, turned quickly, and ran back. "Rump," he said. "Nearly forgot Rump." He disappeared into the yard behind the stone wall for a minute, then emerged carrying the wombat like a fat piglet.

"Oh, for heaven's sake," said Tessa's father impatiently.

"How are you going to handle him?" called Jody.

Mr. Noble was irritated. "You can't carry him like that. If he starts squirming when you're out in the middle he'll have you both down the mine."

"Put him in a bag," Jody shouted.

"Good idea."

So there was another delay while Axel went back to Rump's pen for an old sack. After a short struggle they managed to get Rump into the bottom of it, bulging and whiffling about like a rather lively butt of potatoes. Then they tied the sack tightly with a bit of strong twine.

"Now," said Mr. Noble, "we'll swing him across on a rope."

But Axel was suddenly stubborn. "No," he said. "He goes with me."

A tremendous wave struck the bluff just then and the sound of a sharp crack like a pistol shot came from the tower.

"Hurry up," yelled Mr. Noble. "We both have to get off this devil's marble."

"You first," said Axel. "I'll follow."

Mr. Noble was becoming angry. "All right, then. But hurry."

"I'll be all right."

"You won't be all right, you'll be like an old sea captain, standing on the bridge while the ship goes down."

Mr. Noble crawled back carefully with Axel's bundles

slung over his back. Tessa could see the knuckles of his hands standing out hard and white from the force with which he was gripping the rungs.

"Good work," said the watching men as they reached forward and helped him off the ladders. "Now, Axel."

Axel put the bag in front of him and went down on hands and knees. Then he started to crawl across, shifting the bag slowly bit by bit. It was a dreadful business for the onlookers. Several times he stopped altogether while he adjusted the bag, and once he looked down at the swirling maelstrom beneath.

"Don't look down! Don't look down!" everyone yelled.

He raised his head then like a big shaggy dog, and looked at them.

"Poppycock," he said loudly. "Been a sailor for half my life. Seen lots of places worse than that."

"For heaven's sake don't sit there arguing," Tessa's father blurted out. "Keep going." He looked as if he was about to chew off his fingernails. "Stubborn old porcupine," he said under his breath.

Slowly and painfully Axel moved across, until at last he was within grasp of the hands that reached out for him. They hauled him up and stood laughing and cheering while he lifted Rump from the bottom of the sack and finally stood up, with the wind in his hair and his face beaming. Tessa rushed up to him and put her arms around everything at once—old man and wombat—in a wave of relief and joy.

"You did it, Uncle Axel. I knew you could."

Another huge wave struck the bluff, and then another and another. The monstrous seas that had been whipped up by the storm far offshore were still running in like heaving hills. The bluff shook with the shock of thousands of tons of water trapped in the caverns under the Hammerhead. The sound of their impact thudded and thundered like underground explosions.

There was another sharp crack from the tower, followed by a slow wrenching sound.

"She's going," someone yelled.

They stood mesmerized—half the town of Snapper Bay standing on the cold cliffs in shirts and slippers and aprons and old felt hats, watching the last minutes of a hundred years.

"Poor old Hammerhead."

"What will we do without her?"

"The sea's a cruel monster."

"Look! Look!"

They were all so intent on the tower, gawking and talking noisily, that none of them noticed Axel. He was on the edge of the cliff, staring entranced at the great column with bright eyes and parted lips. He was breathing quickly. For the second time in less than twenty-four hours he was losing a part of his life.

The fall of the tower was so sudden that it caught most of them by surprise. A second or two after another huge sea had sent shock waves shuddering through the bluff, the stonework near the base of the lighthouse suddenly shattered and a gash opened in the curving wall. Then the whole tower seemed to fall sideways, slowly at first but gathering speed rapidly. As it neared the ground it began to break into a dozen huge pieces. The dome-shaped top and the lightroom, with tons of

101

steel and stone and glass, went pitching over the cliff
into the deep water of The Narrows, and the rest of the
column disintegrated with a roar into a frightful ruin of
stone and leaping debris. Several huge chunks bounded
off at odd angles, one of them heading straight for the
canyon in front of the watchers.

"Look out!"

"Back! Back!"

"Run!"

But the piece broke up into bits that went flying down
into the sea before them. For another second or two
there was a plume of dust and falling fragments where
the tower had been standing, but then it was over. The
din of the sea was in their ears, the shattered remnants
in front of their eyes. The Hammerhead Light was gone.

The little crowd stirred and jostled. Tessa moved toward her father. Axel still stood at the edge of the cliff,
staring.

Nobody remembered afterward exactly what happened then, or how it happened. A step to one side,
someone thought, a careless movement, or the effect of
the leaping stones, the frightened jostling of the crowd.
For at one moment Axel was standing there looking
dazed with Rump in his arms, and at the next he was
over the side—not into the newly cut canyon, but down
the rocks near the path that led to the beach, a steep
slope with angles and ledges that dropped away into the
waters of Snapper Bay.

Tessa saw him fall, just a second's glimpse of an up-
flung arm and a shock of white hair.

"Uncle Axel," she screamed. "Uncle Axel."

102

Then she sprang forward, flinging herself down the steep rocks, clambering, clutching, clawing at shelves and niches, sliding, sprawling, tearing knees and fingers till her palms were wet with blood.

"Uncle Axel!" she kept crying. "Uncle Axel! Uncle Axel!"

But it took a long time to reach him.

Thirteen

Axel had a broken pelvis. He had tumbled and fallen, pitched and slid, until he finally lay sprawled on the stones at the edge of the water. Rump had gone down with him, bouncing like a roly-poly bush, sliding and clawing, until he finally shot off a ledge three yards above the shore and plunged out in an arc that took him over Axel's body and into the bay. He was washed up unhurt on the beach a few moments later, whiffling and sneezing and looking pained at having undergone such a sudden bath, especially so early in the morning.

A squad of men carried poor Axel around to the track. There they lashed a makeshift stretcher across the back of the Land Rover and drove him slowly into Snapper Bay. He had to wait a long time then, groaning and half stupefied with pain, until an ambulance could come from Mount Gambier to pick him up. He was given an injection to ease the pain, placed on a new stretcher, and lifted into the ambulance.

Tessa, hovering about in a turmoil of dread, thought

it was cold and unfeeling; Axel had now become a bag of goods instead of a human being, a slab to be slid into the ambulance like a big oven tray. And it was all so sudden. At one instant she was holding his hand and trying to cheer him up; at the next the doors were being swung shut and the ambulance was driving away. No waving, no farewells, no nothing. She watched it dwindle down the street and then turn out onto the main highway.

When it had faded from sight she wiped her eyes with the back of her hand and walked slowly toward the gate of her father's house. She didn't bother to glance down the street again. The town was empty, and so was the whole world.

Axel's injuries were worse than expected. His pelvis was badly fractured, two ribs were broken, and a lung had been punctured. Tessa and the whole family drove to Mount Gambier the following weekend to visit him in the hospital, but there was a mix-up of messages and they missed seeing him altogether because he had just been transferred to Adelaide for special treatment. It was three weeks before they could drive all the way to the city, and then they only had two hours for visiting.

He looked strangely frail on the white bed. They had cut his hair and trimmed his beard so that he didn't even look like Uncle Axel anymore.

"Why did you let them cut your hair?" Tessa asked. "They had no right."

He smiled wanly. "They reckon I was too shaggy. In here they do what they like with you. If they don't like your ears they give you new ones."

She held his hand, lying limp and still as it was on the white covers.

"You'll soon be better," she said. "Then you can come back with us to Snapper Bay."

He nodded. "I'd like that, Tessa girl."

"We'll have a reception ready when you get home."

He looked at the corner of the ceiling, his face fleetingly clouded by something he was thinking.

"Haven't got a home. Have to rebuild the shack first."

"That won't take long. We can build it in a week."

And so they talked, nervously and breathlessly it seemed, with Mr. and Mrs. Noble joining in, until it was time to go. They gave him flowers and chocolates and a book about fishing.

"Look after yourself," they called.

"Not even allowed to do that in here," he answered wryly. "Someone else has to do it for you."

And that was how they left him.

A long time went by. There were complications, and the treatment dragged on and on. Finally, when Axel was ready to be discharged from the hospital, he had to go into a nursing home and then back into the hospital again. Christmas came and went, and the long hot days of January.

Mr. Noble could only afford to drive all the way to Adelaide once a month, and even then the visits were terribly short. And when they did see him Axel seemed listless and unhappy. He was having trouble with his legs and he had to lean heavily on a walking stick.

"He's like an old man," said Jody.

106

"He *is* an old man," Tessa's mother said. "He's nearly seventy-four."

One day a month later, when they were all sitting in the kitchen, Mr. Noble came in with a letter.

"It's about Axel," he said simply, waving the piece of paper in his hand. "They want us to put him in a home."

Tessa looked up sharply. "What sort of a home?"

"An old folks' home."

"No! Oh, no!" She wrenched out the words, looking at her father, wide-eyed and unbelieving. He looked at her kindly and sadly. "I'm afraid there's no other way. He can't come back to Snapper Bay."

She was angry and aggressive. "Why can't he come back to Snapper Bay?"

"Because there's nowhere for him to live."

"He can rebuild the shack."

"He'll never rebuild any shacks. He's an invalid now."

"I'm sure he can. We could all help."

"Even if he could, there's no one to look after him."

"I could look after him."

Her mother turned on her sharply. "Don't be silly, Teresa. In a few years you'll be taking a job, maybe leaving Snapper Bay altogether."

"I won't move. I won't take a job. I'll stay here and look after Uncle Axel."

"Now you're being childish."

"I'm not. I know I can do it."

"You'll get a job, my lass. We'll see to that."

"He needs special treatment, Tessa," her father said quietly, trying to calm the others down. "Someone has to cook nourishing food for him, and give him medicine, and look after him. He'll be much better off in a nice home with nurses and matrons, and other old fellows to talk to."

"Your father's right," her mother said. "Axel's future is in a home. And yours, my girl, is in finishing your schooling and getting a job."

"Then I'll be a doctor or a nurse," Tessa shouted out, "and you know why."

She dashed outside and ran sobbing down the street past the Grand Hotel, past the post office and Mrs. Humble busy with her gossip, past Mrs. Snelling in a new hat, past the rusting crane by the jetty, and so at last onto the wide arc of the beach. She ran and ran, skirting the bay with all its sparkling mirrors, stumbling past the mounds of seaweed, splashing blindly through the ripples and shallows, until she came to the end of the sand and the decaying wreckage of Axel's hut. Still she went on, slowing to a walk at last, climbing the steep track to the cliff's edge and coming out near the windswept ruins of the Hammerhead.

There, at the edge of the canyon that had been newly carved by the sea, she sat down on a boulder and stared unseeing at the wreckage all about her, and sobbed and sobbed. "Oh, Uncle Axel."

For an hour she sat unmoving except for the heave of her shoulders and the shudders that welled up with each new sob. Her eyes were open, but they were as neutral as glass. Yet she saw without seeing, saw things more subtle than knowledge and deeper than sight. Not the world of wind and roaring water, the shattered lighthouse and all the outward signs of men's work destroyed forever. Not the broken fragments of things once thought so permanent, the great rock itself now carved and ravaged into a foreign coastline. But deeper things. Not even the memory of a whimbrel lying dead or a wombat saved, or of a mighty shaft of light pulsing out hope of life to a little ship in peril.

Deeper things. Awareness of a strong man grown old, of the meaning of the tears in his eyes, of the helplessness of men and women to put a stop to time, to keep sickness and pain at bay, even to help each other when the days for parting came. Awareness of the joy of sharing, of times when the mornings ran with laughter, of days when the sunshine lay like warm gold across the land. And of the certain loss of these things that now lived on as a hurt in her heart, a loneliness that was hers alone.

But at last her sobbing eased and she stood up, pressing the palms of her hands into her eyes and smearing the tears on her cheeks to make them dry in the wind. Then, with a last look at the Hammerhead, at the torn and savaged wreckage of the great rock and the tumbled ruin of the Light—all this that was now like a strange place—she turned and went back down the steep path behind her.

A few minutes later she emerged on the beach.

Then she walked slowly back to Snapper Bay.

Format by Gloria Bressler
Set in 11 pt. Century Expanded
Composed by The Haddon Craftsmen, Scranton, Pa.
Printed by The Murray Printing Co.
Bound by The Haddon Craftsmen, Inc.
HARPER & ROW, PUBLISHERS, INCORPORATED